Sherlock Holmes A Baker's Dozen Demise

Sherlock Holmes Trilogy, Volume 1

Don Henwood

Published by Don Henwood, 2021.

A
Baker's
Dozen
Demise

By Don Henwood

This book is a work of fiction. The names, characters, places, and incidents described in this novel are the product of the author's imagination or used fictitiously.

In the style of Sir Conan Doyle, I have used Watson's narrative to begin the story as Doyle had done in some of his writings.

However, Isambard Brunel is an actual person who had a remarkable career as a civil engineer. I am using his name to tip my hat to him and his accomplishments.

Book 1: A Baker's Dozen Demise
Book 2: The Anatomy of Sherlock Holmes
Book 3: Blood Thicker Than Water (spring 2022)
Novella: Sherlock Holmes/ Letters from Jack

Deep into that darkness peering, long I stood there, wondering, fearing, doubting, dreaming dreams no mortal ever dared dream before—Edgar Allan Poe.

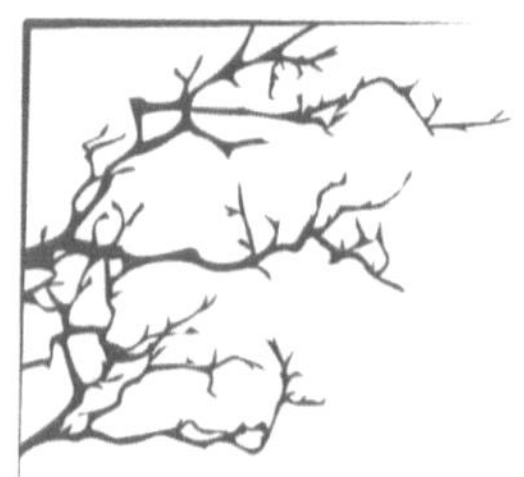

Prologue

A notebook in my lap now contains the essential details of our latest adventures. Closing the book, I put my Dixon pencil back into my breast pocket and see Sherlock Holmes staring out the window into a featureless dark landscape as our train travels through the open country between Bristol and London. The hour was late, and there was little to distract ourselves with. Holmes had spent most of his time in the dining car, but he had returned when a party of men became too noisy over a game of cards. I could see he was still restless.

"Holmes, it's been a long day. I could dim the lighting if you would like to try to sleep," I said.

"No, thank you, Watson. My blood is still up, and sleep would be impossible." He stood and shrugged on his coat. "I think I'll have a smoke between cars. The fresh air will do me good." He left without inviting me to join him.

By the time Sherlock Holmes had returned to their compartment, Watson had stretched out on one side of the benches with the lights dimmed just enough for Holmes to settle in when he came back.

"I'm not asleep if you want to talk," I said from under the hat covering my face.

"Thank you, but that's not necessary. We're only about an hour out from Kings Cross Station. I will wake you when we arrive." Holmes dimmed the lights further and sat by the window on the other bench.

I peeked out from under my hat and saw Holmes's silhouette like a black marble statue.

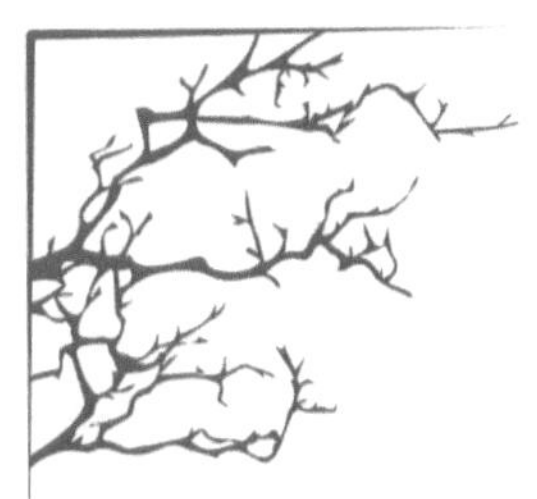

Chapter One

An insistent knock woke me from my pleasant slumber. A dream, now fading into the mist of consciousness. My eyes still closed, willing the intruder away.

Rap-rap-rap, the knock invades again with an all too familiar voice, "Watson. Watson. Are you awake? I need to speak with you."

I opened my eyes to a darkened room with drawn-tight drapes. It felt as if I had been sleeping only a few minutes. My limbs were leaden and sore from traveling.

Sherlock Holmes and I had just returned this very evening from a harrowing case that took us to Bristol. Our week-long pursuit led us from the city's cultured center to the rough and dangerous wharves along the River Avon. But we accomplished our mission with the return of the Eastern Orthodox religious Icon owned by the Isambard Brunel family.

Upon our return, and, as often as it was his tradition, Holmes lit a warming fire in the sitting room and found comfort in his fireside chair with his pipe in hand. But I felt near exhausted. I said my good night to Holmes and retired to my room to catch up on a much-deserved rest.

"Watson." Holmes's voice rose with renewed urgency.

"Give me a minute, Holmes," I said as I threw off my covers and hung my legs over the edge of the bed, my feet hitting the cold, bare wood floor.

While still in the dark, I could hear his footsteps moving away from my bedroom door to other parts of the apartment.

The chilly floor sent a shiver up my spine before I could find the slippers, my toes prodding the length of the bed. Then, I wrapped myself into my robe that hung on the foot rail. My hands fumbled blindly for the box of matches on the bedside table, and when found, I lit the single candle in its stand. There was not a hint of daylight filtering through the drapes to give me a clue of the hour. A sigh escaped involuntarily, sensing the hour was still predawn.

Why did Holmes wake me at such an ungodly hour? Truth be known, this wasn't the first time he had roused me from sleep. Sherlock Holmes wasn't a respecter of civilized times. He lived in his world with his own rules. To be his friend, one had to adapt to his lifestyle and respond to his beck and call at the most inopportune of times or circumstances.

I left my dark cocoon to find the sitting room empty. Holmes was nowhere to be found. "I'm up," I called out, turning to look at the Swedish grandfather clock—it was a present from the House of Bernadotte. (A scandal averted by Sherlock Holmes' investigative talents.) The hour hand was pointing at the Roman numeral two. I could not help but yawn at the realization.

"Holmes," I said with a bit of ire in my voice. "You've awakened me in the middle of the night, and now leave me to stand here and wait?" My hands were set on my hips like a scolding mother, but there was no witness to be seen.

"Sorry, Watson," Holmes said as he came out from his bedroom door. "I need to have a word with you."

"So you say. I think I'm awake enough to converse." I notice Holmes is clothed. "Dressed already, Holmes?" I asked.

"Never undressed, Watson. I just now returned. While you slept, I was called away." Holmes's voice was bright and alert.

"Lestrade, I asked?" expecting no relief from the demands put upon by Scotland Yard.

"No, nothing so interesting. It was a message sent from the Diogenes Club. Mycroft had requested a meeting with the greatest of expediency and had sent a coach to be at the ready."

"Must be serious," said I.

"Nothing of the sort," said he.

Sometimes, I felt like getting Sherlock Holmes to answer my questions was like pulling teeth from the jawbone. And at other times, he'd ramble on like an incoming tide that couldn't be held back.

I asked, somewhat exasperated, "Then why the early summons, Holmes?" Another yawn escaped, and my jaw was wide open.

"We must pack at once. There is no time to waste," Holmes said.

I stretched out a kink in my neck. "If that is what you wish, I'll have my bags packed shortly. But can you give me an idea for how long?" My friendship with

Holmes never questioned the sanity of his requests, but I was often left in the dark about the details.

"Three weeks at the minimum. We sail later this afternoon," Holmes said, turning back to his room at a swift pace to continue packing. "There is a carriage waiting at our doorstep. Now hurry."

Left with limited information, I packed comfortable traveling attire, assuming we would spend most of our time on trains and multiple forms of carriages. And all too often, traipsing through bramble and brush, regardless of the weather.

I FOLLOWED SHERLOCK Holmes as we quietly descended the stairs and exited two-twenty-one-B Baker Street. We climbed aboard the curbside carriage with its twin brass oil lamps lit, giving off a subdued glow. "I'll have these bags loaded and tied in a jiffy, governor," the driver said.

Then came a careless thud as he tossed the luggage upon the platform and the leather straps cinched. The carriage rocked as the driver mounted to his seat. With a crack of the whip above the ears of the two coal-black horses, the cab jerked forward, and they sped off into the night.

I took off my hat and gloves and then asked, "Where are we heading to, Holmes?" I assumed we were crossing over to the Continent when Holmes had told me we would be going by ship.

"America. New York, to be specific." Sherlock Holmes could not see my surprised expression but heard a brief gasp.

"What intrigue sends us there?" I asked inquisitively.

"No intrigue, my friend. On the contrary, we're nothing more than errand boys," Holmes said with a hint of disgust in his voice as he took out his pipe, slid down the window, and tapped out the remains of an unfinished smoke.

"Come now, Holmes. It can't be as bad as that. I take it has something to do with Mycroft. And I'm sure he would never ask if he didn't have a good reason. Please, tell me all."

Sherlock Holmes finished packing the bowl of his pipe in a ritualistic manner. He then struck a match from the bottom of his shoe, lighting up the cab briefly and drawing in a few quick puffs. He blew out the flame with a cloud of smoke, and his face was hidden again in darkness.

Holmes was ready to begin, "Though I argued every point, Mycroft said only I could be trusted to represent him, and therefore, her Majesty's Government on a delicate negotiation." I heard a snort coming from Holmes. A first that he could ever recall.

Holmes continued, "I said there must be a hundred men who could run his errand. However, he emphatically stated that he depends on my analytical skills to ferret out any duplicity in the agreement. And I replied, isn't that what lawyers were for? But before I could raise another objection, Mycroft handed me an envelope with our tickets and a Letter of Authorization representing him and Her Majesty's Government. Then, declared we barely had time to catch the morning train and would hear no more of my objections." The constant crimson glow of Holmes' pipe was the surrogate for his unstated displeasure.

I peeked out the curtained window, seeing the building's dark silhouettes passing by. "I can understand your brother's faith in you. But why the cloak and dagger business? Why on such brief notice and under cover of darkness? None of this makes sense."

Holmes reopened the window, tapped out the used ash, and tucked his pipe back into the inside pocket of his jacket. "Mycroft is concerned that those who disapprove of these negotiations will try to sabotage the agreement. He waited until the last possible moment to enlist our help. Thus, we are to take the morning train to Liverpool. From there, we will take a cab to the harbor and remain in the carriage until the final boarding. Then, we'll come aboard our passage on the Servia."

"All right. Now I understand Mycroft's reasoning for sending you. But why me?" I asked, still puzzled.

Holmes said matter-of-factly, "He concluded you would be willing to accompany me to New York if for no other reason than to keep me from throwing myself into the sea." Holmes paused a moment, then said, "And that is a direct quote."

I burst out laughing, "He knows you all too well, Holmes. And I'll try my best not to disappoint him."

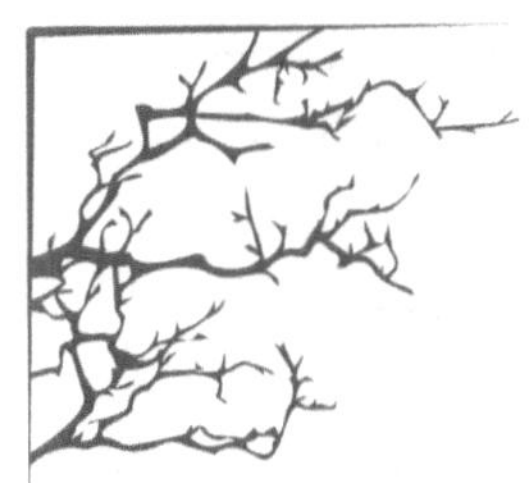

Chapter Two

At this early hour, the train platform's activity surprised Watson. The train from Liverpool had only arrived here a few minutes earlier, and people were still coming out of the rail cars. "Holmes, it never occurred to me that workers would use the train to come into the city for their employment."

"Did you assume all goods and services originated in the heart of our metropolis?" Holmes asked.

"To tell you the truth, I'd never given it a thought. Everything we have ever needed has always been at our disposal and close at hand." Watson said with a new sense of wonder.

"It's good to see your horizons have expanded, Watson. Shall we board now?" Holmes answered with a chuckle.

Holmes and Watson sidestepped several passengers exiting and gave their baggage to the nearest porter. "This way, Watson," Holmes directed him to their assigned car.

With a call from the conductor, a cloud of steam, the train would leave the station at four-o-seven with a sparse outbound ridership. A short whistle burst from the locomotive, and with a jolt as its wheels turned, the train car couplers stretched and clanged with the grind of scraping metal.

Holmes and Watson jostled through the corridor until they found their assigned compartment. They entered their private space, closing the door and locking it behind them. Mycroft had purchased all the seats, giving them complete privacy.

Earlier, the incoming commuters had filled almost every space, and crews were behind in their clean-up. The train had also been late in arriving at the station, and only now were they moving through the compartments, sweeping and picking up the detritus left behind.

As Holmes and Watson settled in, a porter came to clean their compartment but found the door locked. "Excuse me, I'll just be a moment, sirs," he said from the passageway.

"You need not bother," Holmes said as he closed the curtain.

"Holmes, where are your manners?" Watson asked.

"Mycroft implicitly instructed us not to contact anyone until we were on the ship. He made it quite clear; no one was to be trusted."

"Does that mean we won't be going to the dining car for breakfast?" Watson asked with a frown. His empty stomach was already growling its demands for satisfaction.

"Let me ask you: when you worked in a field hospital in Afghanistan, did you ever go without food for a day?"

"Of course. But back then, I was much younger," Watson said, smiling since it had only been a few years ago.

Holmes slowly shook his head. "You'll survive." Then Holmes put his feet up on the cushions across the aisle, tilted his hat over his eyes, and said, "If I know my brother, we'll have a splendid meal on the ship. Until then, I'm sure you will survive."

WHEN THE TRAIN ARRIVED in Liverpool at Three-fifty-seven pm, Sherlock Holmes and Dr. Watson gathered their luggage, departed the train, and headed away from the platform. The winds came off the ocean with a moist crispness, chilling to the bone.

A short, stocky man with gray mutton chops and wearing a heavy red and yellow Mackinaw jacket approached them, saying, "Mr. Holmes, your brother has sent me to pick you up."

"And why should I trust you?" Holmes said suspiciously.

"Well, sir, Mycroft told me to tell you, the busy bee has no time for sorrow. Whatever the hell that means."

Sherlock Holmes turned to Watson, "Mycroft had instructed us to go with the person who gave me this code phrase." Turning back to the man, he says,

"Lead on then." After being on an overheated train and not acclimating, they were now both anxious to get out of the cold.

"This way, gentlemen. The carriage is just around the corner," the man said as he walked away, leaving them to carry their bags.

A highly lacquered black coach with polished brass trimming stood at the ready. Two harnessed snow-white Arabians nodded their heads as if they were passing greetings in a parade. Watson commented, "I think I will enjoy traveling in style." He elbowed Holmes in jest.

As the two men climbed aboard and shed their outer coats, Watson noticed a wicker basket covered with a two-person red and black checkered blanket sitting on the floor. He picked the blanket up and wrapped his and Holmes's lap, tucking it in on his side. He then lifted the basket onto his lap while looking inside the container. "God bless Mycroft; he's thought of everything."

Dr. Watson took out a loaf of dark rye beard, Havarti cheese, sliced roast beef, a bottle of Merlot, and a small basket of strawberries and cream in a corked bottle. He laid them across the bench seat like a buffet table in front of their laps. At the bottom of the basket were the necessary implements, plates, silverware, and a cutting knife.

Watson's eyes almost sparkled, "Despite what you said earlier, a well-fed military travels better on a full stomach." Watson proceeded to dish up a heaping plate of food while Holmes was content with a slice of bread and cheese.

Though the carriage ride to the harbor was not very long, Holmes and Watson would remain behind the closed curtains for another hour and a half, glad for the blanket covering them.

Dr. Watson had taken his time with his repast. He finished his last sandwich and sipped on his wine when a quiet knock came rapping on the outer door. "It's time," the driver said. He then climbed up, led the horses a quarter mile down to the docks, and stopped in front of the Servia's gangplank.

From their vantage point, the ship's red and black hull looked massive; she was an impressive five hundred and fifteen feet in length. Topside, her barque-rigged sails remained bound while in port, but the coal-fired engines were in service, belching smoke through her stacks and ready for departure.

"What a beautiful piece of engineering," Watson said as he stood in awe.

"The vessel is newly launched, and this is her second voyage across the Atlantic," Holmes said. Watson marveled that Holmes would know such details, but he usually did.

A ship's porter met them with a luggage cart and helped the driver unload while Sherlock Holmes and Dr. Watson ascended the ramp. The Purser stood at the top of the ramp wearing his spotless uniform with gold bands on his cuffs. He greeted them with a smile and looked at the tickets Holmes had handed to him.

"Yes, sir. Your stateroom is on the top deck, port side. That would be on your left, sir." He said with a practiced smile.

Holmes held his tongue from some sarcastic retort, knowing this young man had given these same instructions hundreds of times today. Turning left, Holmes led the way with Watson at his heel and the porter bringing up the rear, pulling the cart behind him. The stateroom keys were in the door lock, and though it was chilly, they had cracked the windows open for fresh air.

Sherlock Holmes entered the suite and took off his coat. "If this is how our Government wastes money, then we shall be broke before the turn of the century," He stated to Watson as if lecturing at the University.

When Watson came through the door of their first-class suite, he saw adjoining bedrooms, a sitting room with high box-beamed ceilings, a crystal chandelier, and a small marble surround fireplace. A fire had already been lit and warmed the room to an entirely acceptable temperature.

Watson pulled off his shoes and lay on the long sofa facing the fireplace. "I don't know, Holmes. I could get used to this," he said as he reached for an apple sitting in a bowl on the low table in front of him. "I'm looking forward to what's in store when we sit at the table in the saloon this evening."

"I shudder to think, Watson. I fear neither of us has brought proper attire to be seated if these accommodations are any indication of what's coming. We should have known Mycroft's appetites would tend to run in these directions. I would have preferred steerage over this; much easier to blend in, you know."

Watson took a bite of his apple as he put his other hand behind his head, propping it on the sofa's armrest. "Well, we'll just have to suffer through it and make the best of it we can."

Holmes saw the smug grin on Watson's face. "It's been a long day for me, Watson. If I don't come out in a few hours, please wake me." Holmes left Watson with his apple in hand and a smug smile on his face.

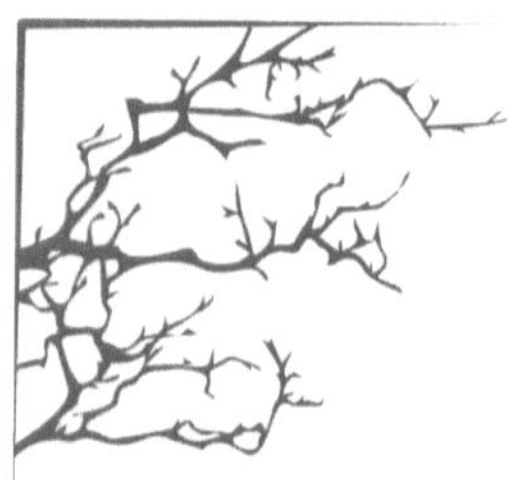

Chapter Three

Sherlock Holmes was awake, dressed, and shaking Watson by the shoulder, who was still softly snoring into the sofa pillow. "Watson, my good man."

Dr. Watson's eyes fluttered open, "Did I fall asleep? I was resting my eyes. What time is it, Holmes?"

"Time to dress for dinner," said he.

"I'm sorry, Holmes. I have already failed in my assigned task. How would I have explained to Mycroft that you had jumped overboard even before losing sight of land?"

"Let's see how dinner goes before I make that decision," Holmes said as he walked back to his room.

"That's it, Holmes. Keep a stiff upper lip," Watson laughed.

Sherlock Holmes returned with his pipe and struck a match on the fireplace's brick liner. "Humor only goes so far, and Mycroft wouldn't be pleased to find out you were the cause of my abandoning ship."

"Point well taken. I'll try to keep it a silent vigil from now on, Holmes." Watson said as he chuckled. "I'll dig into my bag and see what I can come up with to make myself presentable."

When Watson returned, he was wearing a pair of black trousers, a Callahan frock coat in charcoal, a gray and white stripe waistcoat, and an English square silk tie. Smiling, he said, "Will this do, Holmes?"

"I'm afraid anything less than white tie and tails will be out of form, but we've done our best, and it will have to do."

The fire had died to the point of embers, and neither bothered to stoke the flames with fresh coal. Holmes opened the cabin door and ushered Dr. Watson through. Then, following him out, he locked it behind them.

Sherlock Holmes was not quite ready to go to the saloon and face the inevitable. "Let's take a breath on the promenade. A short walk will whet our appetite."

"That is a Splendid idea, Holmes. I have eaten more than I intended from the basket, and I wouldn't want to miss out on a proper dinner. First-class dining is an opportunity not to be missed," he said while rubbing his hands with pleasure.

They climbed a single flight of stairs and exited the stairwell, pushing hard on the windswept door to open it. They stepped out into a stiff breeze as the vessel cruised along at sixteen knots. The bow cut through the ten-foot swells, rising precipitously on each crest. Holmes and Watson inched ahead into the wind, holding onto the handrail to keep their footing.

Shorebirds had long since abandoned their escort and returned to the English shoreline and their cozy nests. And the sun began to set, hidden behind a layer of clouds to the west. It appeared they were the only ones topside, much too cold and challenging for most first-class travelers.

As they neared the stern on their second lap, Sherlock Holmes leaned in close to be heard saying, "Take a look behind you. We're being followed."

Watson glanced back, "You mean the steward that appears to be polishing the rail with a dirty cloth in his hand?" Watson smirked. "And in the middle of rough seas?"

"Yes. I saw the steward at the end of the hall when we left the room. Then he came out the same door several minutes after us. He doesn't appear to be doing any chores on deck, and his rail polishing is spaced few and far between. Besides, who in their right mind would work out here without a coat?"

"Should we confront him?" Watson asked.

"No. If it's a coincidence, which I doubt, it will mortify him. But if he's following us, I'd rather not tip our hand. We'll have to see." Holmes shuddered from the chill, "I think it's time to head to the saloon."

Watson blew on his gloved hands, "About time, I'm freezing."

Holmes and Watson entered through the stern doors and descended the stairs to the main level. Through the aft doors, they passed by the smoking room with Morocco leather seats. A pleasing scent of tobacco lingered near the entry. Continuing down the corridor, they entered the vestibule, where the grand stairway stood majestically, as ornate as any hotel in England.

Across the foyer beside the saloon entrance, a man dressed in formal tails, a bright white shirt, and a black bow tie held a brown binder at his side. He greeted the guest with a smile and a slight bow at the hip.

Dr. Watson and Holmes loitered at the foot of the stairs, watching the dinner guest approach the Maitre d'. The passenger guest names were checked, and entry was granted. The table server led each party to their assigned table.

Holmes adjusted his tie and pushed a hand into the outer pocket of his dinner jacket, trying to look casual. "Watson, I'm afraid we can't delay it any longer." Holmes was not looking forward to this evening's ordeal.

As they approached the saloon's entry, the maitre d stepped in front of them, sizing them up with a sour look. "The dining room for steerage is one floor below this deck. If you'll go down those stairs," he pointed the way with a crooked finger. I think you will find your names on their list. I'm Holmes, and my associate, Dr. Watson."

Nonplussed, Holmes said, "I believe you will find our names on your dining list. Sherlock Holmes and Dr. John Watson."

The Maitre d' indulged Holmes by opening the leather-bound ledger and running his finger down the guest list. His hand motion stopped, and a startled expression grew on his face. Stuttering, he said, "I... I apologize, sir. I have made a terrible mistake. Please let me lead you and Dr. Watson to your table." Watson was curious why the man was so apologetic.

Several heads turned towards them from the seated diners as they watched the small procession to the center table. Sherlock Holmes whispered to Watson, "Not exactly, inconspicuous." Watson quietly smiled at Holmes' apparent discomfort and answered Watson's question.

The round center table had placards set at each setting as Holmes found his name card and pulled the chair out. Watson sat to his left. On Sherlock Holmes' right sat a middle-aged woman, apparently with her husband beside her. Her neck was bejeweled with three rows of pretentious diamonds. The placard read Mrs. Blake. "Hello," she said, drawing the word out like an opera singer and drawing her lips into a circle.

"Good evening," Holmes said, hoping not to engage. He turned his head away and saw Watson was about to speak with the young lady sitting beside him.

"Good evening," Watson said to her.

Her quiet voice responded, "Good evening," as she leaned towards Watson to see the name card, "Dr. Watson."

"John, please." Watson beamed a warm smile.

"John, it's Emily Anderson. I am very pleased to meet you." She held out her small silk-gloved hand, petite as a willow shoot.

"The pleasure is mine, Miss Anderson," Watson said as he took the offered hand. "Are you traveling alone?"

"Please call me Emily. And no, I have a chaperone accompanying me. But they did not give her the first-class passage. So, she is dining in the women's drawing room just down the hall. But I think it's a rather silly rule. After all, she shares the suite with me."

"May I ask what brought you to England? Your American accent gives you away."

"Yes, my Boston accent, I have been told, is almost too hard to understand. But then, I could say the same about some of the English. There were places I traveled; I couldn't understand a word they were saying," she smiled innocently at Watson.

John laughed. "It all depends where you're at in our country. I must admit, there are times when I'm outside of London, and generally, up in the north, I have to ask people to repeat themselves. You know, they roll their R's like a drum." He smiled at this engaging young woman.

"Oh, you mean Scotland?" she asked.

"Both Scotland and Ireland. English isn't really their native language. I'm sure if they had their druthers, neither would speak an English word again, much less ruled by the Queen."

Emily's eyes brightened as she laughed softly, "In answer to your question, I was the lead dancer in a production of Swan Lake. I have been traveling for the last two months through your beautiful country." Emily glanced at the ceiling with a dreamy expression, "But now, the fairy tale has come to an end, and I turned in my glass slipper. But alas, I return home to continue my education at Boston University."

While they had been talking, they now had three more seats occupied at their table. An elderly couple that was obviously upper-crust English. They introduced themselves as Lord and Lady Kingston of Hardwicke. "Please, while we are on this trip, do call us Charles and Caroline," said the husband with a laugh. "My wife wanted to go on the maiden voyage, but unfortunately, I came up with a case of shingles, An awful bother at that." Charles suddenly looked stricken, "Perhaps that was too personal."

Mrs. Blake's attention was drawn away from Holmes to the new couple. "I do sympathize, Charles. Our chef had it, and it took him the better part of two months to recover. But I see you look fit as a fiddle now." Lord Kingston smiled at the American woman's audacity.

The third person joining the table across from Lord and Lady Kingston addressed the others: "Good evening. My name is Ethan Caldwell, Former Ambassador to Belgium. I look forward to getting to know each of you during our time onboard." His attire suited his former position. This man shined in these social settings, making eye contact with each person seated, especially with Miss Anderson.

Holmes was familiar with Ambassador Caldwell. He remembered reading about him losing his wife during a fox hunt at Balmoral Castle three years ago. Her horse attempted to jump a fence, but its rear leg caught the rail and fell on her. Holmes could see the ever-present pain in his eyes despite the smile he wore like a mask.

There remained one empty seat yet to be filled, which was about to be resolved. Sherlock Holmes watched an officer in a white uniform with black bands on his cuffs making his way toward them. He stops at a few tables while greeting the guests. Then came to their table and sat down in the vacant chair.

"Good evening," his voice was strong and commanding. "My name is Captain Johnathan Starr. Welcome to the Servia."

There was nothing Sherlock Holmes enjoyed about this evening. All the secrecy in the planning, only to have him displayed in the midst of the first-class snobbery, was like an organ grinder's monkey holding a cup out to collect coins from the audience—and at the Captain's table, no less. Mycroft might as well have had him waving a flag and declaring his mission.

"So, Mr. Holmes. What brings you on this voyage, business, or pleasure?" Mrs. Blake asked as she tugged on Holmes' sleeve and leaned in too close for his comfort.

Holmes was definitely not one for small talk. Nor was he willing to lie outright. "I'm representing my brother in a business negotiation," he said as his eyes wandered the room.

"How interesting. Do tell me more," she said, leaning even closer. Her breath was potent with the smell of alcohol.

"I'm not at liberty to discuss the matter," Holmes said, hoping to cut off the conversation.

Mrs. Blake spoke as if in shared confidence, "My husband is the editor for The New York Times. I guess it's in the blood; we're always looking for an interesting story."

"What's that, dear?" Jack Blake asked, leaning in front of his wife. The alcohol was so pungent on his breath that Holmes arched back in his chair.

"Mr. Holmes is traveling to New York City on business. Very hush, hush." Mrs. Blake babbled.

Mr. Blake slurred his words as he said, "Mr. Holmes. If you need an introduction to the business community, I can help," his chest puffed out at his perceived importance. "In fact, I'll invite you to The University Club. Nothing happens in Gotham City that doesn't start there." Jack Blake then folded the newspaper he had been reading before dinner, rude by any standards to be reading at a dinner table.

Sherlock Holmes caught sight on the front page of the Times. The heading read Dead Doctor Dies Dramatically printed in bold letters.

"Mr. Blake, are you finished with the newspaper? I hadn't had a chance to pick one up before boarding," Holmes asked.

Mr. Blake exhaled a noxious breath, "Be my guest. It seems to be mostly cricket scores and horses. I never could understand how you limeys ever became a world power."

Mrs. Blake lightly slapped her husband on his arm with an embarrassed laugh, "I don't think people like that term, dear. Now, you apologize to the nice man."

Mr. Blake cleared his throat and handed the paper to Holmes, saying, "Sorry, chap. Perhaps I've had a few too many high-balls before dinner."

Holmes received the paper and was fortunate the meal was brought forth at that awkward moment. Thus ending an annoying conversation.

Holmes kept to himself as the dinner guest chatted about nothing. His distaste for these settings grew with each passing minute. And the moment the meal was finished. Sherlock Holmes took Watson by the elbow, saying in a whisper, "Watson. Let's have a brandy in the gentleman's smoking saloon." Holmes rose and left without further delay, leaving Watson to make their apologies.

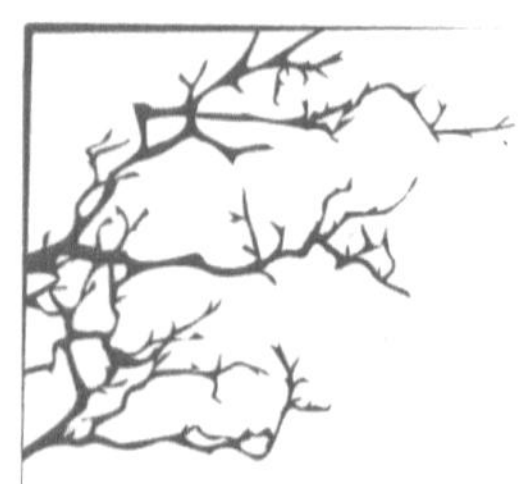

Chapter Four

Sherlock Holmes opened the newspaper with his pipe pressed between his lips, a trail of smoke rising to the ceiling, a brandy at his side, and sitting by a blazing fire in the smoking lounge.

The article he began reading was an account of a gruesome murder at Dr. Matthew Elliott's home, situated off Bishopsgate Street in the city of London.

According to an unnamed source, the doctor was killed with a scalpel from the doctor's private antique collection. It was stated that the perpetrator had scrawled a series of words from the victim's blood on the library wall. This was witnessed by the butler, who found the body when the servant brought the morning tea. However, Scotland Yard said the message was not being disclosed to the public at this time.

It was further stated that none of the house staff had heard any commotion during the evening. The butler was the last person to see Dr. Elliott alive at approximately ten thirty-five p.m. There was no sign of forced entry, but the Police refused to confirm.

Scotland Yard declined to comment, stating they had not examined all the evidence at this time. This reporter saw the lead Inspector, Inspector Lestrade, as he accompanied the body to the coroner's wagon. When asked, Lestrade refused to say a word, keeping the public in the dark.

"I, for one, question our community's safety when someone of this stature is murdered in their own home, and Scotland Yard just sits on their hands. It's time to raise our voices and demand action."

"Holmes, what has got your attention? I swear you haven't breathed for the last minute," Watson said, leaning forward in his chair.

"I'm not sure. For a moment, I felt someone walking over my grave. I can't put my finger on it. But never mind." Sherlock Holmes fell back into silence and stared into the fire, leaving his brandy untouched.

Watson sank deeper into the leather wing chair, holding the snifter near his nose. He breathed in the woody scent of his brandy before saying, "Miss.

Emily Anderson seems a delightful young lady. I'm only sorry I hadn't seen her perform." Watson waited for Holmes to respond, but he didn't reply. "I said..."

"I heard you, Watson. But she's almost half your age." Holmes continued to stare forward.

"Really, Holmes. I only spoke to her for a few minutes. It's not like you to jump to conclusions. And besides, it's less than ten years difference." Watson sipped on his drink to hide the color in his cheeks.

Holmes turned to Watson with the leveled look he gave when he was about to reveal a case. "You're an eligible bachelor, a doctor in good standing. And I suppose women probably find you attractive. It is a very reasonable assumption." Holmes paused a moment before adding, "You seemed to take quite a shine to her."

"But as you said, she is very young and an American no less." Watson lifted his head and grinned at the ceiling. "Though she would be stunning on my arm at the opera, I would think."

Twenty minutes later, the after-dinner crowd began filtering in, and within fifteen minutes, the room felt stuffy. "It's getting late, Watson. I'm going to our cabin." Holmes stood waiting for Watson to reply.

Watson finished the last of his drink and set the empty glass on the table. "I'm coming with you." He thoroughly understood Holmes' disdain for elitist nonsense.

SHERLOCK HOLMES OPENED the door and let Watson in. He scanned the corridor in both directions, looking for the steward who had been watching them. Someone had turned the room lights on, and the fire had stoked to a hardy blaze. The fire starter tinder box was full, giving the room a hint of pine aroma.

"Definitely, I could get used to this," Watson said, loosening his tie.

"Good night, Watson," Holmes said as he headed towards his suite.

Dr. Watson had decided to have one more nightcap before retiring. He poured a whiskey from the bar, moved a Queen Anne chair close to the fireplace, and removed his tie, waistcoat, and shoes before taking his seat.

Sherlock Holmes came back out of his room and said, "We have been rifled, my dear Watson."

"What? What do you mean?" said I.

"I was retrieving an item from my drawer and noticed they slightly rearranged my clothing. Someone has been through my possessions, and there is evidence of tampering throughout the room."

"Did they take anything?" Watson asked, then realized it must have to do with their mission. "Are you carrying documents to the United States?"

"I am," Holmes said.

"Are our lives in danger, Holmes?" Watson asked, now concerned.

Sherlock Holmes joined Watson with a drink and sat in the other Queen Anne chair. "It's nothing that dramatic. I have a proposed agreement between our government and a contractor from New York."

"I think it is time for you to tell me the complete story. Are we talking corporate espionage?"

"Let's start from the beginning, my good man." Holmes drank half his whiskey and soda before saying, "Mycroft believes we are at the dawning of a new age. Take this vessel as an example. Here, we sit under electric lights. We are traveling on the first liner to cross the Atlantic with this luxury. The coal-fired boilers that power the ship also turn the turbines, creating electricity."

Holmes set his unfinished drink on the mantle. "Our government wants to encourage the development of electric utilities throughout England, starting with the conversion of our streetlights."

"As incredible as that seems, who could object to modernizing the city," Watson asked.

"Coal-gas. There is a monopoly on this asset. A limited but influential group of men controls it. Even though they would be the ones who supply the coal for the power plants, they oppose the change."

"Why in the world would they do that?"

"Think of the supply lines. Miles and miles of piping run through our streets. They have a considerable investment that returns stellar profits. Coal gas is a byproduct and of limited value other than burning it. It would behoove them to retain the status quo. Thus, taking these documents and delaying the contract allows them more time to influence the Parliament."

"If that is so, what do you propose now, Holmes?"

"The person who searched through our cabin is a professional and will assume our lack of detection. He and or his accomplices will gain access to the ship's vault, expecting to find the documents safely locked away. In the meantime, we'll keep watch." Holmes stood, stretching his arms behind his head and yawning. "Good night, Watson." Holmes left his friend to contemplate the evening.

Watson marveled at how Holmes could remain so composed in situations like this and wondered what it would take to fluster Sherlock Holmes.

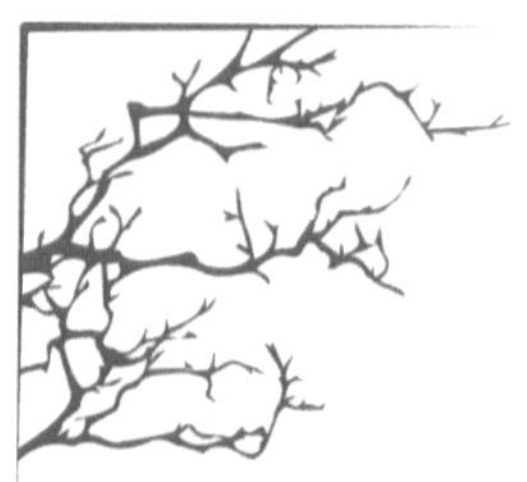

Chapter Five

All seemed quiet over the next five days. Holmes and Watson settled into a routine of early morning walks on the promenade when the weather permitted, followed by a late breakfast in their suite. Both found quiet corners in the smoking lounge to pass the day as the ship sailed ever westward.

Watson laid his copy of The Brothers Karamazov on the side table and crossed the room where Sherlock Holmes was sitting. As he came near, he thought to himself, what a creature of habit Holmes has become. Sherlock Holmes sat with his feet propped up on an ottoman next to the fireplace. His pipe and awful-smelling shag tobacco lay on the table next to him. And he had that far-off look, the same as when analyzing a case for hours at a time.

Watson moved a chair close to Holmes, "You have to admit this is quite an acceptable way of travel."

Holmes slowly turned his head toward Watson, "I'll grant you this: having quiet time to read and reflect is restorative. But I find the conversations during dinner at the captain's table utterly laborious. You haven't noticed because you're distracted by Miss Anderson."

"I'm sorry, Holmes. I've managed to fail yet again. I promise to be more attentive." Watson moved to the edge of his seat. "Holmes, why do you suppose the...?" Watson searched for the right word. " The spies, thieves, I don't know what to call them. Why haven't they made any more attempts at acquiring the documents?"

Holmes' gaze returned to the fire. "Who says they haven't? Someone has reexamined our suite twice, and they tried to pick my pocket just last night."

"They did?" Watson exclaimed in surprise. "How do you know this?"

"As for our accommodations and not to give away all my secrets," Holmes chuckled. "I use a simple technique of placing a single hair bridging two drawers or door and casing. If they have been parted, then I know they have compromised the room," Sherlock Holmes had a glint in his eye. "I know what you are thinking. Could it be the maids coming in to change the sheets and bring fresh towels?" Watson began nodding. "I leave the markers when we are dining in the evening. It is the only reasonable length of time to search our rooms without worrying about detection. As for the pickpocketing. Do you recall last night when we were heading to the dining room, and a man who appeared drunk stumbled into me while another man brushed by at the same moment?"

"I do. In fact, I reprimanded him for his inappropriate behavior." Watson then thought, "You still have the papers on your person? If so, how is it they came up empty-handed?"

Sherlock Holmes gave a wry grin. "The documents are not in any of my pockets." Holmes stood up, glanced around the room, and unbuttoned his shirt's last three buttons, revealing a wrap. "I'm using a tensor wrap."

"That's ingenious, Holmes." Watson looked puzzled. If they have made all these attempts and come up dry, they only have another day left to acquire the papers. Will they not become desperate and make a bold move just before docking?"

"No. I don't think so. They will wire for further instructions once we get ashore. After all, they are not common thugs. If violence were their plan, I would be floating somewhere out on the Atlantic long before now."

"Ha. Then I would have been in trouble with Mycroft for sure," Watson laughed.

"Well, Watson. One more night to bear. One more night to put up with the insufferable prattle." Holmes sighed audibly.

"Let's exchange seats tonight. I'll act as your barrier wall between the American couple. I haven't completely missed the cues."

"It's a generous offer, Watson. And I appreciate the gesture. But there is no point in causing a conflict. The Blake's may be uncouth, but they would feel offended by the slight." Sherlock Holmes reached into his side pocket and removed his timepiece. Holmes spoke as if proclaiming a death sentence, "Speaking of which, the hour has come."

Watson nodded reassuringly, "I'll be right with you, Holmes. Let me get the book I have been reading. It's a new book by Dostoevsky. I only hope I can finish it before we dock tomorrow."

Holmes and Watson entered the dining room for the last time and were escorted to their table and seated by their server. Within minutes, they filled all the other seats around the table except for the Blake's, which was unusual. Their habit was to come early and mingle with the other guests.

Watson and Miss Anderson talked in hushed voices until the Captain approached the table and said, "The Blakes will not be joining us tonight. I'm told Mrs. Blake has come down with a migraine headache. Our thoughts go out to her for a speedy recovery." Watson turned his gaze to Holmes, who looked almost sheepish as if it were his fault.

"John," Emily said to Watson as she placed her hand on his left arm. "I feel so bad for Mrs. Blake. When I get too tired, I often get dreadful headaches that last all day. I tried cold compresses and shutting the drapes. But with the schedule they had me on, I mostly suffered through them. A stagehand once offered me opium. He said it would cure it in minutes. But my mother would have wrung my neck if I had even entertained the thought. What do you prescribe to your patients?" she asked with a demure smile.

"Well, working with Sherlock Holmes keeps me busy. I haven't practiced medicine since the Afghan war, but I do try to keep up with what's new. I recently read an article about a French chemist who has had remarkable success with a Salicin compound for pain relief. Short of that, a hot bath and brandy will generally do the trick for me." Watson was keenly aware of her hand's placement.

"I'll keep that in mind. But the brandy will have to be hidden in my closet. My mother is a teetotaler."

Lady Caroline Kingston waved her hands to get the attention of everyone at the table, saying, "All week, I have wanted to tell you of our plans when we arrive in America, but Charles has dissuaded me until tonight. He kept telling me no one would care, but I'm just too excited to hold it to myself."

Captain Starr smiled and said, "Then, by all means, good lady. Do tell."

"Though it's obviously winter, once we arrive in New York, we'll board a train heading west. Our destination is a week in the new National Park at Yellowstone. There's a lodge there that we'll sled into and be up to our chins in the snow. I have never been in more than an inch or two of snow all my life. I have dreamt of this for years. And Charles is hoping to see a buffalo before they are extinct."

Emily Anderson clapped her hands in delight. "Lovely, absolutely lovely. We get lots of snow in Boston, and I love every minute of it. There is nothing more enjoyable than getting bundled into a pile of blankets and driving through the open countryside in a horse-driven sleigh." Her eyes almost glowed, and those at the table joined her in the flight of fancy with nodding heads and bright smiles.

On this last night of the voyage, the dinner guests ate a lavishly prepared meal. At its conclusion, buckets of iced Champagne were carried by the wait staff through the kitchen door.

While the crystal glasses were being filled, the Captain stood waiting for the room to quiet. "Ladies and gentlemen, the Cunard Line, the crew, and I want to thank you for sailing on the RMS Servia. We will dock tomorrow morning, sometime around ten. If you have not already secured transportation, there will be coaches for hire waiting nearby. But for now, I toast you." The Captain held his glass up and turned a full circle to a room of appreciative smiles. "For those interested, we shall have live music and dancing in the music room aft. For you, landlubbers, that's at the back of the ship." The Captain sat as the guests clapped with laughter and appreciation.

Watson leaned toward Sherlock Holmes and whispered, "Holmes..."

"You needn't ask. I'll return to the men's lounge until you say good night to Miss. Anderson. Besides, I'm reading a rather thought-provoking study of botany by Swedish botanist Carl Linnaeus. I suppose it will take several more hours." Holmes smiled at Miss. Anderson. "Good night, Miss Anderson."

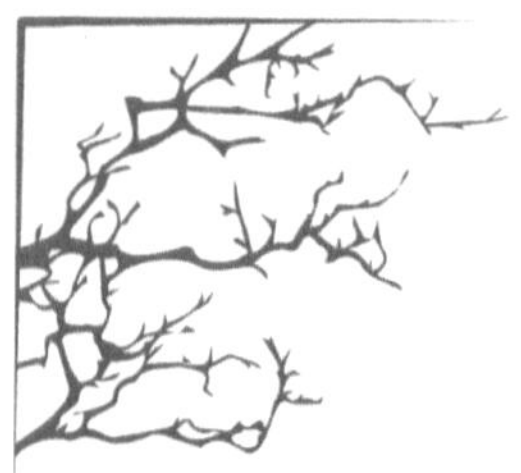

Chapter Six

Dr. Watson climbed into the carriage after Holmes had settled. The driver had their luggage strapped on in a few minutes and came to their door. "I'm all set, gentlemen. Where are we going?"

Before leaving London, Sherlock Holmes had memorized the instructions, "You will take us to The Hoffman House on Broadway and twenty-fourth."

"Yes, sir. I know it well, a splendid establishment, finest in the city." The words made Holmes cringe inside. Once again, Mycroft's pomposity for selecting accommodations for the wealthiest of gentlemen put Holmes and Watson in the spotlight.

The moment the carriage fronted the hotel, two porters dressed in light gray overcoats descended the steps; one came to open the door while the other began unloading the luggage. As Holmes and Watson approached the entry door, the doorman drew it open and tipped his hat. Warm air gushed out like Sahara Desert winds, warming them even before stepping inside. "A bit chilly today," the doorman said in greeting. "But fortunately, we haven't gotten our usual December lake-effect snow. When that happens, this city comes to a standstill."

Holmes didn't need to reply to this triviality; instead, he moved directly towards the front desk. A tall, pale man whose limbs could be mistaken for a human willow tree gave a per-functionary smile and spoke in a falsetto voice. "How may I help you?" he said while he glanced at Holmes' sub-par attire.

"You have our reservations, Sherlock Holmes and Dr. John Watson," Holmes said.

The desk clerk looked disapproving, just like the Maite d' on the Servia did as he scrolled his register. Surprised, he said, "I do have your reservations made by your British Government," he looked again at Holmes, trying to make sense of the scenario. "Your rooms are two-twelve and two-thirteen." The clerk signaled the porter with a glance to lead the guests to their rooms. "One moment. I have a note in your box," he reached up to the pigeon-hole shelf and got the key and sealed envelope, handing them to Holmes.

The porter led them up a broad set of stairs covered in an oriental weave pattern rug with brass rods bracing the treads. The hall had the same carpet, and they spaced plant stands every few doors. Photographs of the New York City skyline hung throughout the corridor.

After the porters left Sherlock Holmes and Watson, Watson knocked on the communicating door. Holmes opened his side, and Watson came through. "Not bad, Holmes, not bad.," Watson said as he moved to the window to look outside. "I never imagined that New York City could be as bustling as London. I can't wait to experience what she has to offer." Watson turned back into the room. "Have you read the note yet?" Watson asked as he walked over to a counter with a crystal decanter holding sherry. He poured two glasses and held out one to Holmes.

"I was just about to open it when you knocked." Holmes took the offered sherry and sat on the powder-blue silk sofa as Holmes tore through the envelope with his pocketknife. A cream-colored page, folded in thirds, slid out into Holmes' hand. Unfolded, Sherlock Holmes first read it to himself before sharing it with Watson. "It is instructions for me to meet with my counterpart tomorrow afternoon in the hotel's bar at four pm sharp." Holmes sipped on his drink, "Watson, I think it's time for you to carry your sidearm from this point onward. I don't expect any trouble in the hotel bar, but by tomorrow, the saboteurs, for lack of a better word, will probably have received explicit instruction on how to handle this affair."

"I already have it in my pocket," Watson said as he withdrew the gun to show Holmes.

"Oh, and Watson, if you must see the city tomorrow, please be back by two. We'll take lunch here in the hotel and see if we are being watched and by how many. I personally have no interest in being a tourist and will remain here in my room until you get back."

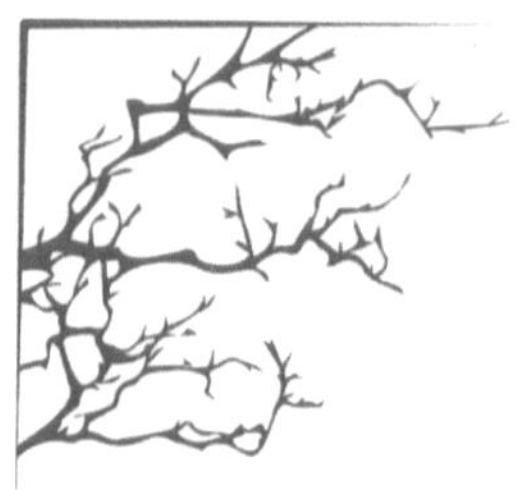

Chapter Seven

atson joined Holmes for breakfast in Holmes' room. A silver serving tray sat on the table with a pot of tea, a pot of strong coffee and freshly made scones wrapped in cloth within a basket and all the necessary condiments to go with them.

"Tea and scone," Watson lamented. "Do you ever very?"

"Why would I?" Holmes retorted as he buttered his first scone.

"We are in a different country. You could try something new." Holmes looked at him blankly and grinned before picking up the daily newspaper.

WATSON ARRIVED BACK at the Hoffman House a few minutes after two and rushed in to meet Holmes. He weaved between tables while removing a new pair of gloves and unwrapping his scarf. His face flushed from the sub-freezing temperatures, and his hair tousled from a bitter wind. By the time he reached Holmes' table, a waitperson had intercepted him. "I'll hang your coat for you, sir," the waitperson said with formality.

Watson looked around and realized no one had a coat, either worn or hooked over the chair. "Yes, quite, my good man," he said as he recovered from his faux pas.

Watson pulled out an upholstered chair and sat across the table from Holmes while letting out a rush of air as if he'd been running. He still had his gloves in hand, having forgotten to give them to the waiter with the coat.

"It's a remarkable city, Holmes. New buildings are going up everywhere. I walked by one in the financial district that was fourteen stories. And they even have a subway system much like London's." Watson began looking around the restaurant, hoping to order a drink. "Take a look at these gloves," Watson said as he handed his pair to Holmes. "The sign on the display counter said they were made from Texas longhorns. Though, I'm not exactly sure what that's supposed to mean." Watson finally caught the eye of their waiter and waved. "The store had several floors and departments with a three-story courtyard. I purchased these at Lord Taylor's, just a short walk from here. I believe there might be a similar store by that name in London."

"Are you ready to order?" Holmes asked, seeming disinterested in Watson's report.

"Almost. I have one more thing to add. I walked by a store called Macy's and couldn't believe the street window displays; they were very commercial. It looks like presents are a substantial part of the Christmas season here in America."

A waiter came to the table, ready to take their orders. "Will you be joining Mr. Holmes for lunch?" the server asked, seeing that Watson hadn't looked at the menu.

Watson didn't even pick up the menu, saying, "I'll have whatever Holmes is having." After the server left, Watson asked. "So, what are we having?"

"Moussaka." Watson looked confused, not knowing what that meant. Holmes smiled and took pity on him. "It's made with either eggplant or potatoes with minced meat and a Middle Eastern sauce. I ordered it with the potato, a slight variation on our English meat and potato dish. After all you just said this morning, I should venture out on my dining selections." Watson sighed and gave a look of relief, resolving never to challenge Holmes' diet preferences again.

Watson noticed Holmes was distracted and thought it was because he was a few minutes late. "How long have you been sitting here?" Watson asked.

"Long enough to locate the same three men who were on the Servia. Two of them are sitting at the table in the far back, just under the last window. The third is on the eighth stool at the bar. He's watching us using the mirror behind the counter."

"What are we going to do?" Watson asked.

"I'm going to eat lunch and then retire to my room until the appointed hour."

Watson laughed, "Then, in that case, I'll have an American beer to go with my meal." Watson felt like he could finally relax.

AT FOUR O'CLOCK, SHERLOCK Holmes walks into the bar. The high ceiling electric chandeliers are ablaze, casting shadow specters. The room is crowded and stuffy. A thick layer of tobacco smoke hovers over the patrons like a London fog, and their voices compete to be heard over the din.

Holmes looks for the man who, per his instructions, wears a brown bowler hat with a red satin band. He elbows past a group of men standing near the door and sees the gentleman sitting at a square table with four straight-back chairs but only one seat occupied.

He scans the room, quickly identifying the three men who remained on his tail. It appears there is no need to hide his meeting. Somehow, the opposition knew of every plan made. That meant there had to be an inside man. Someone close to Mycroft has been leaking information.

Holmes approached the table, looking the man straight in the eyes. "I'm Sherlock Holmes."

"And?" the man said, returning the same stare.

"The busy bee has no time for sorrow," Holmes repeated the code phrase, sat in an empty seat, and leaned across the table. I'm sure they have made you aware of individual parties' attempts to derail these negotiations." Holmes gave a slight nod towards the two men sitting at a distant table in the corner of the bar. As we speak, they are still trying to keep us from an agreement. And they have three agents in this room watching us now."

The man chuckled, "Mr. Holmes, American business isn't above using cutthroat tactics, but it's all part of the game. You Brits take things too seriously. I'm well aware of influential men in London who stand to lose substantial profits. It's not a question of if, but when change comes to England. Our task, Mr. Holmes, is to come to a mutual agreement that your government will find acceptable."

Holmes straightened back up in his chair and took a bundle of papers from his jacket pocket. "With that in mind, here is Her Majesty's proposal," Sherlock Holmes said. He laid his government's proposal on the table and slid it over to the other party.

Jason Clark, Executive Vice President of Edison Electric, took the papers and studied them for a few minutes.

"Well, Mr. Holmes. We're not that far off from coming to terms." He reached into a satchel and brought out an envelope. "I anticipated what your offer would be, and I have prepared a counter-proposal for you to consider." Mr. Clark held out the manila envelope and passed it to Sherlock Holmes. "In my communications with your brother, Mr. Holmes, he said I couldn't fool you with legal doublespeak. So, I've saved us both time and effort by being straightforward. To be honest, sir, we want this contract as much as your government. Though this project is minor in scale, it portends the future. And hopefully, a long profitable agreement between our countries." Jason Clark picked up the beer mug near his right arm and took a drink.

"Our countries?" Holmes questioned.

Laughing, Mr. Clark said, "Whatever is good for Edison Electric is good for the United States."

Holmes started to open the envelope, saying, "Let me take a look at them."

"No, no, Mr. Holmes. Please read our proposal at your leisure. I suggest we meet here again, same time tomorrow?" Jason Clark stood, extending his hand to Sherlock Holmes. "I have Christmas shopping to do."

Watson watched the conversation from the entry area, adding his smoke to the hovering cloud from a cigar he had purchased at the bar. He also kept watching the men who had been following them, the saboteurs waiting for their chance. Every once in a while, he'd feel for the revolver in his right-hand pocket. It gave him a sense of reassurance.

After Mr. Clark shook hands with Holmes, he left the bar. Sherlock Holmes waited a minute, then quickly stood and walked towards Watson. The three men left their positions and came to intersect Holmes. On cue, Watson walked past Sherlock Holmes and bumped into the nearest two men, allowing Holmes to depart the bar and disappear into the crowd. "Oh, excuse me," Watson said as he brushed by.

WATSON SAT IN HIS ROOM, listening for Holmes' return. The chime on the clock sitting on a cabinet signaled a quarter past nine. Watson poured his third sherry of the evening, worried that Holmes wasn't able to elude his shadows. He wasn't pleased with Holmes' plan and would have preferred staying at Holmes' side, strength-in-numbers. But when Sherlock Holmes set a course, he was the immovable object.

Coinciding with the half-hour chime, a voice from the other side of the communicating door said, "Watson, are you awake?" Watson almost laughed. How often had he heard that very question asked in this same manner? Or was it his overwhelming relief that Holmes was back?

"Coming, Holmes," Watson rushed to the door, forgetting the sherry on the counter. He joined Holmes on the sofa and sat on the other end. "Well, are you going to keep me in suspense or tell me what happened?"

"Your timing was perfect, my good, Watson. I got into the coach waiting outside and was gone before they reached the door. The driver took me to the Western Union Telegraph office on Dey Street. Once inside, I conveyed the counter proposal and told Mycroft that I found it most agreeable. He told me the opposition has gathered strength, and having this signed and returned is needed to quell any further protests. He told Lord Brixton the agreement was already signed and on its way. I disapprove of lying to a member of Parliament, but that is not within my discretion. I also informed him of a mole within his inner circle."

"What now? They're still at large and looking for their opportunity?" Watson asked.

"All in good time, Watson. All in good time."

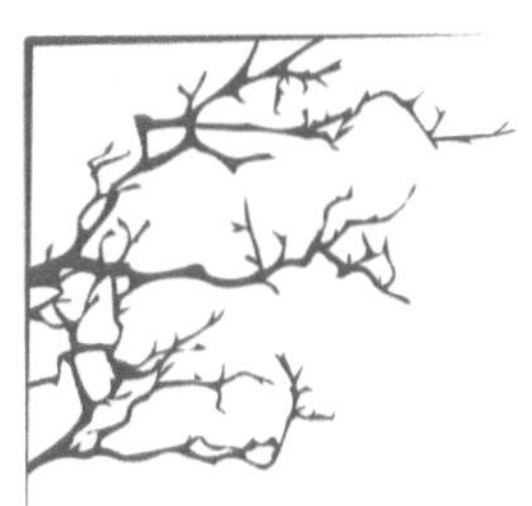

Chapter Eight

After another evening of further negotiations on the finer details, they brought both parties to an agreement. They drew the papers up, and a final meeting was to occur at the same location, same time, and the same table.

JASON CLARK HAD A FOLDER lying on the table in plain view when Sherlock Holmes entered the bar. "Good evening, Mr. Holmes. I've taken the liberty of ordering you a brandy to celebrate."

"Thank you, Clark," Holmes said as he lifted the offered glass in a toast. "Shall we finish our business?"

Jason Clark took out a small teak box sitting by the folder. He opened it and brought out a black fountain pen and ink well. Clark dipped the pen and put his signature on two copies of the contract. When finished, he turned the folder to Holmes. "Here you go, Mr. Holmes."

Sherlock Holmes signed as the British Government's representative. "Mr. Clark, have you made the arrangements I suggested?" Holmes asked.

"Yes, I will be escorted from this establishment with four guards hired from the Pinkerton Detective Agency. And you, Mr. Holmes?" Jason Clark asked.

At that moment, Watson approached the table and took a seat. Holmes said, "May I introduce my associate, Dr. John Watson."

"Pleased to meet you, Dr. Watson." Jason looked slightly confused, "After what you told me, isn't one-man insufficient protection? What do you intend to do now?"

Sherlock Holmes grinned, "I intend to go have a nice dinner out," he said as he finished his brandy.

"Well, good luck, Mr. Holmes," Mr. Clark said with a questioning look. "I hope we will meet again when I come to England to start this project." Jason Clark shook hands with Holmes and Watson and left with four powerful-looking men in tow.

"Holmes," Watson said, "he has a point about protection and you are requesting I leave my revolver behind. Now you say we're going out to dinner. Please tell me you haven't lost your mind." Watson said as he scratched his head in confusion.

Holmes laughed, "Have I ever steered you wrong, Watson?" Holmes gave him the look—you've got to trust me. "I saw a splendid-looking bistro just down the street a few blocks. Let's give it a try," Holmes said louder than needed. Two of the shadow men quickly made for the exit, even before Holmes and Watson stood.

By this winter hour, the sun had long since set as Holmes and Watson left the pub. They found that modern city streetlights were lit with electric lighting that was brighter and crisper than London's faithful gas lights. The pedestrians were few and far between, and a scattering of carriages whisked their rides to appointed destinations.

Holmes set a casual pace as they walked along the street. "Watson, don't be too surprised when we get to the alley up ahead. I expect us to be assaulted by the men who have been following us. This is their last opportunity to relieve us of the documents. That is the reason I asked you not to bring your revolver tonight."

Watson was taken aback, "How are we to defend ourselves? We're outnumbered."

"My dear Watson, I don't intend to defend ourselves. I expect that other than being jostled, they have no plans to harm us. They want the contract we signed ten minutes ago. As I said earlier, even a temporary delay in Parliament could achieve their goal. Mycroft had told me their support was gaining strength, and without an agreement soon, they would succeed."

By the time Sherlock Holmes had said this to Watson, they were about to pass by the alley. Two men stepped out of the darkness with boards found in a scrap pile. A third man appeared from the shadows behind them, saying, "Do as I say, and we won't have to bash in your heads," the man ordered, trying to sound menacing.

He took Holmes and Watson by the arms and led them into the dark alley, out of sight of any potential witnesses. "Check their clothing everywhere," the leader said, "he won't fool us again." Rough hands pulled at Holmes' clothing as they went through his pockets. He then yanked off his overcoat and jacket, searching through each thoroughly. The searcher even pulled up Holmes's shirt. "Ain't nothing here," the man cursed under his breath.

To the assailant's surprise, they came up empty-handed. "Where the hell's the contract?" the leader swore at Holmes.

Sherlock Holmes smiled at them, saying, "Too late, gentlemen, I have passed the contract on and is on its way to England."

Dumbfounded, the three men stood with their hands limp at their sides, at a loss for what to do next. Suddenly, the ally lit up as waving lanterns rushed in from both directions. "Stand where you are and drop those weapons, or we'll be forced to fire," said a police officer from the New York City Police Department.

"Your timing was perfect, Officer Hawkins. I will leave you to decide what to do with these men, and I will bid you a good night," Holmes said.

"That was a gutsy move, Mr. Holmes. They could have done severe damage before we could have come to your rescue."

"Not at all, Hawkins. Their specialized occupation has no violence. They're not common thugs. You could tell by how they held their boards; they were bluffing. So, again, good night, sir." Holmes said this as he led Watson out of the ally and continued his walk as if the event hadn't happened.

HOLMES OPENED THE DOOR of the Bistro to let Watson pass. The pleasant smell of seared beef wafted through the diner. The restaurant was busy, and one table was left near the kitchen door. A burly waiter built like a wine barrel and wearing a multi-stained white apron waved them in the direction of the lone table.

"I'm sorry, this is the only spot left. Sit down, and I'll bring a bottle of wine to your table." The waiter returned with the red wine and two glasses a moment later. "I don't think I've seen either of you here before. Let me tell you how this works. We serve only one dish each night, family-style, something I picked up working out west," he paused to let that sink in. "Tonight, we're cooking Porterhouse Steaks with Cajun plank chips. The red wine is a Merlot, cheap, but there's no limit. That is unless you two get unruly."

Holmes and Watson looked at each other, weighing their options. Then Holmes leaned back in his chair and said with a smile, "When in Rome. Aye, Watson."

THE FOLLOWING DAY, Sherlock Holmes sat at the small table in his suite, having breakfast he had ordered from room service. While reading the New York Times, he shook his head in amazement while reading American political antics and their outlandishness. Holmes thought to himself, 'How can a powerful country be so unruly?' A soft knock on the door drew his attention and him away from the paper. He moved to the entry door and opened the small square viewing box. A young boy stood with an envelope in hand.

Sherlock Holmes opened the door, and the youth said, "I am sorry to disturb your breakfast, Mr. Holmes. This telegraph just came to the front desk, and the messenger said it is urgent, sir." He handed the sealed envelope to Holmes while tipping his hat and backed away.

SHORTLY BEFORE TWO, Holmes could hear the familiar movements in Watson's room. He knocked on the door and said, "A moment, Watson. I have something to tell you."

Watson came through the adjoining door, "Holmes, I just came from Central Park. What a magnificent haven in the midst of a bustling city." Watson noticed that the entrance to Holmes' bedroom was open and saw the luggage packed and lying on the bed. "Are we going somewhere, Holmes?"

"I received a wire from Mycroft this morning. Lestrade came to his office seeking our whereabouts. Something has Lestrade in a dither and needs our return posthaste. Mycroft has booked passage for us to return, and we leave in three hours."

"What a shame; I was just enjoying this city." Watson thought for a moment or two, "What does Lestrade have to do with this case? Did he have grounds to arrest the mole?"

Holmes shook his head, "No, Mycroft is dealing with that person in other ways. Lestrade came searching for me. He had exhausted all the usual channels and was at his wit's end. After explaining his reasons, Mycroft relented and told him of our mission. There appears to be some urgency in Lestrade's request. He told Mycroft the clock was ticking."

Watson asked, "What does that mean?"

"Watson, you know my brother. The only thing he is economical with is his words."

Dr. Watson laughed, "I must admit, he did go overboard on our travel accommodations. But never let it be said that I'd find fault with traveling in style." As Watson turned to leave, he said, "I'll be ready when you are, Holmes.

"Good. I'll go downstairs and ask the desk clerk for a carriage and have a porter come get our luggage."

WATSON AND HOLMES BOARDED the ship just before five. They stayed in the same first-class accommodations on the same vessel that had brought them across the Atlantic four days ago.

At dinner that evening, Watson made an observation, "Holmes, the couple that was sitting over at the table near the window. I could swear they were on the trip over with us. But he had snow-white hair and a thick white beard. And she looked at least twenty-five years older."

"Watson," Holmes said with a laugh. "I have trained you well. Your observations are correct." Watson looked confused. "They are part of Mycroft's team, our bodyguards, in case we get into real trouble. My dear fellow, we were never really in any danger."

Watson considered that for a minute before stating, "They were the ones you passed the contract to when we left the bar. I distinctly remember that you brushed by them on the way out the door."

"Yes. It was never a plan for us to be on this vessel with them. Mycroft wanted to keep the contract and the saboteurs apart. But with the events of last night, that is no longer an issue. But I'm sorry, Watson. I know how much you would have enjoyed staying in New York City for a few more days."

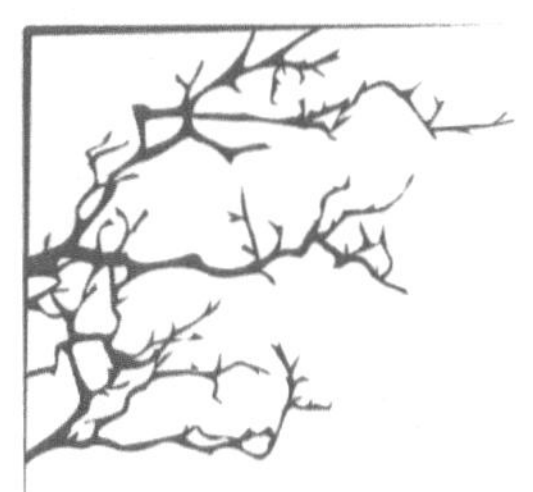

Chapter Nine

"Holmes, you seem to be much more comfortable traveling in first class," Watson pointed out on the second day.

Holmes was sitting on the sofa, his legs planted on the tea table while holding a cup of Earl Grey steaming in his hand, "Not being indentured to Mycroft helps, and not sitting at the captain's table with the upper-upper crust. It almost gave me indigestion. I always feel better when I can blend into my surroundings," Holmes said with a relaxed sigh.

They had settled into their previous routine and no longer needed to be looking over their shoulders. Holmes still spent most of his time doing laps on the promenade, even on those occasions that it snowed. He also spent long hours in front of the fireplace in the gentleman's lounge. Watson was used to these periods when Sherlock Holmes drew into himself. But this also allowed Watson to entertain himself with some of the ship's conveniences.

Watson wasn't a good pool player, but he wasn't bad either. He had played more pool these last three days than in the previous ten years. To make it a bit more interesting, Watson found other passengers willing to play for a few shillings a ball. If Watson had done a tally, he would have been up by six shillings, not exactly a career to be had.

It was nearing seven, and he expected Sherlock Holmes to come through the door at any minute. Watson had a run of three balls going and a decent spread on the table. He was lining a shot by using the wall for a bank shot. Bent halfway over the table, Watson slid his stick back and forth three times, eyeing where exactly he wanted to make contact, a centimeter or two to the left. Watson struck the cue ball, putting a slight spin on it and sending it across the table. Unfortunately, the shot was too soft, and the number five ball ricocheted off both bumpers, ending an inch away from the pocket.

"Nice try, Watson," Holmes said from the doorway. "Do you suppose you could finish up after dinner?"

The other player said, "That works for me. My wife hates it when I'm late, and she has to carry the conversations at the table."

Watson suggested, "Put your billiard stick on the table so we don't forget who has the next shot.

"See you after dinner, Dr. Watson. I'm still two shillings behind." Holmes and Watson left the man at the table while he finished his whiskey.

FOR THE FIRST THREE nights of their voyage, Holmes and Watson sat at a table set for four. However, each night, one seat remained vacant. Watson had been the one who principally engaged with the third diner. The man was in his mid-forties, with a full head of salt and pepper hair. From the look of his tanned and weathered skin, he had spent a great deal of time in the outdoors.

Watson asked, "Sooner or later, one gets around to asking this question, and that's your reason for taking this trip?"

Mr. Sheldon nodded his head with a smile. The words were on the tip of his tongue when another man came to the table. He pulled out the chair and lowered his flabby bulk onto the cushion. This person exuded a rotten countenance and a sour smell. All three men immediately disliked him.

"Where is the damn waiter?" the man shouted towards the kitchen. Turning to face the others, he said, "For the service we get, these people are overpaid." No one at the table responded.

"John, I was about to answer your question. I'm returning to England to spend Christmas with my father."

"Wonderful," Watson said. "How long has he lived in England?"

Angus Sheldon burst out laughing. "Well, that confirms it. I've lost my accent. You see, my father has always lived in England. And I did, too, until I turned twenty. I didn't want to end up working in the same factory as my father and his father and his father. So, America seemed the best choice." He stopped and looked at the other at the table. "Am I talking too much?" Angus asked.

Watson put up his hands, waving them, "No, no. Please go on."

"Mr. Holmes?"

"By all means, continue." Holmes leaned back in his chair to put a bit more distance between himself and the obese man.

"I found work cutting timber in a logging camp in upstate New York. One day, the cook served pancakes with syrup. That was the first time I had ever tasted maple syrup. I started asking questions about where and how it's made. That was the beginning of my love affair with the heavenly liquid."

"The following year, when my contract expired, I packed everything I owned on my horse and headed north. I ended up in Montpelier, Vermont. I bought a sizable plot of land covered in maple trees with the savings I hoarded. For the better part of twenty-five years, I have harvested, manufactured, and marketed my brand of maple syrup. If you have had syrup on this ship, you were eating Angus Syrup. Except for a couple of years, there hasn't been a day that I haven't walked among my trees." Mr. Sheldon laughed again, "Now you know my life's story."

Sherlock Holmes leaned forward with that look that Watson knew well. "Perhaps there is a bit more to add. You have been a horseman all your life. And when the War Between the States started, you joined the First Cavalry Regiment. You were wounded in the right knee during the war, either the kneecap or somewhere very close. And finally, you keep your own books."

Angus Sheldon threw up his hands in amazement, "How do you know these things, Mr. Holmes?"

"Mostly observation, my good man. Your gait shows you are bull-lagged. You have a slight limp with a small catch in your walk, indicating an old wound. I formed a composite from your and Dr. Watson's conversations over the last three evenings. You're mentioning that the gap in time was the last piece of the puzzle. As a man of honor, you would have volunteered for service during the War Between the States, and the cavalry would have suited your abilities. And finally, a person who keeps extensive accounts tends to acquire an ink stain on their thumb and index finger. Though faint, I detect traces embedded in the swirls of your skin."

Before Angus could respond, the heavyset man said with a huff, "Parlor games. You play parlor games. If you are so acute with your reasoning, tell me something about me?"

In Holmes's face, Watson could see that Sherlock Holmes weighed whether or not to answer. And he wouldn't have, except for the man's haughty glare.

"You, sir, were born into a family of great wealth but have not contributed a penny to it. You have not worked a day in your life and traveled extensively to avoid the issue. Though you try to give the impression of nobility, your actions indicate otherwise. I'd say your family's wealth comes from being industrialists, probably coal, judging by how you treat others as inferiors. I can tell you are on an allowance, excessive by most standards, but you manage to squander it quite easily. You play cards and lose often. When your money ran out, you started handing out IOUs, but even now, the other players suspect you will renege on your obligations. Thus, your ban from the table and the reason you're sitting in that seat."

During this monologue, the man's face turned several shades of red, and his bulldog jowls quivered with rage. He blew deep breaths like he was trying to blow up a balloon. "I will not sit here and be insulted by the likes of you." He stuttered in cohesively, unable to make his retort. Instead, he stood tipping over his chair and stamped out of the saloon, saying, "From now on, I'll be dining in my suite."

Dr. Watson and Angus Sheldon sat, stunned. An awkward moment passed before Holmes said in a low voice, "I should not have said those things to him, deserving or not."

Sherlock Holmes was not accustomed to emotional support. He flinched when Watson placed his hand on Holmes' shoulder. "Holmes, you spoke the truth to an awful man. That anyone can plainly see."

"It doesn't make it right." Sherlock Holmes cut into his beef and, when finished, sat quietly for the rest of the meal.

Angus asked, "Can I buy you, gentlemen, a brandy after dinner? I think we all could use a stiff drink."

THE THREE MEN GATHERED around the smoking lounge fireplace with drinks in hand. "Mr. Holmes," Angus said, "I, for one, applaud what you said at the dinner table. A man like that is the very reason I left England." Angus Sheldon opened his jacket and brought out a silver case. Inside were a half dozen wrapped cigars. "Mr. Holmes? Dr. Watson?" he held out the silver box to each person.

Watson reached for the matchbox with the Cunard Line logo on the mantle and struck a flame. When they had their cigars well-lit, Angus began pacing back and forth in front of the fireplace.

"As I told you before," Angus began, "our family has worked in a factory for many generations. The conditions in which they work are deplorable. Profits are the only concern for the owners. And the workers are no more than enslaved people in their eyes. They're kept in poverty by design to ensure compliance. Perhaps one day, the unions will gather the strength to oppose these tyrants." Angus's voice rose with the last sentence. Then, in almost a whisper, he said, "That man is a blight on society."

Sherlock Holmes stood, placing his empty glass on the mantle. "Good night."

After Holmes left, Angus asked, "Will he be alright?"

"Yes. Holmes has a short fuse when it comes to pomposity. But by tomorrow, he'll be right as rain. Now, would you care to join me in the billiard room? I was in the middle of a game before dinner."

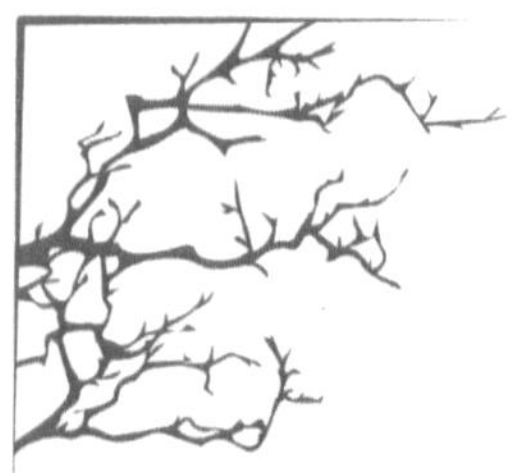

Chapter Ten

The Servia docked in Liverpool at its appointed time of 10 p.m. Unfortunately, they had missed London's last train by a half-hour. Holmes and Watson would need to find suitable lodging near the train station and keep their luggage packed for an early departure.

Sherlock Holmes and Dr. Watson took a hansom to the train station to check the morning schedule. Holmes asked the driver, " Would you please wait with our luggage on board? I don't think this will take too long."

The station platform was empty and dimly lit. Holmes entered the station and approached the ticket counter, where a middle-aged man sat on a stool behind a flimsy grate. His back turned away, and he was reading The Illustrated London News.

"Excuse me," Holmes said.

The ticket-taker jolted from his seat and came to the counter. "I'm sorry, sir. No one ever comes to the counter at this hour. How can I help you, sir?"

"Dr. Watson and I need tickets to London for the morning. And, if you don't mind, directions to a hotel nearby."

"Yes, sir, I can help you with both." He wrote out two tickets and handed them to Sherlock Holmes. Then said, "There is a friendly and quiet hotel a few blocks down Crown Street. That will be one pound-six apiece, sir."

AT SEVEN THE FOLLOWING day, Watson rose to find Holmes already gone. He stayed in his nightshirt and ordered coffee and scones from room service, knowing he still had almost two hours before the train's departure.

After his second cup of coffee, Watson dressed, expecting Holmes to rush through the door at any moment. As if on cue, Holmes returned as Watson finished the knot on his tie.

"Good, you 're dressed, Watson," Holmes said as he spotted the scones on the table. "Do you mind?" Holmes eased over to butter a still-warm pastry.

"Where have you been off to at such an early hour," Watson asked.

"The telegraph office. Mycroft wanted to know of our safe return. More importantly, his agents return with the contract. Once we dispensed with that formality, he wired back that Lestrade was desperate for our return. But then, there is nothing unusual about that." Holmes helped himself to another scone. "I have a boy with a luggage cart coming in fifteen minutes. Do be ready, Watson." Holmes went to his room to freshen up.

Sherlock Holmes and Dr. Watson walked in front of the cart, heading the six blocks to the train station. Though it was cloudy, the marine air kept the temperature mild for this time of the year. But it also created an air inversion, causing the coal smoke to sit heavily over the city.

Watson noticed Holmes was very quiet as they strolled along. "Holmes, what are you thinking? You're more quiet than usual."

"The future, Watson. What we accomplished over the last couple of weeks may seem insignificant on a larger scale. But think about how life will change as we develop the use of electricity. I'm not talking about streetlights. Someday, homes will be wired. And I believe we'll develop other power sources other than using coal. Can you picture London without its brown haze?"

"My Holmes. Never thought of you being so philosophical."

"Visionary, Watson, visionary."

SHERLOCK HOLMES WOULD not have admitted it if asked, but sitting in a train compartment with all the seats taken was less comfortable than their trip to Liverpool. What made matters worse was that they ticketed a young mother with two children for their compartment, and a very obsessed man occupied the last seat. Unfortunately, they had assigned seating and could not change locations.

Holmes had purchased a morning paper before boarding and tried his best to read it. Watson watched him from the seat directly across, but the news sheet hid Holmes's face. The child who sat next to Holmes swung his arm back and forth and struck the paper several times. Watson could see Sherlock Holmes was clutching the edges and wadding them in his fist.

Watson could not hold back a smile, thinking Holmes was definitely not reciting the scripture -"suffer little children to come unto me-." In fact, Watson couldn't remember when he'd ever seen Sherlock Holmes interact with a child other than the Baker Street boys and speculated on how long Holmes could put up with this inconvenience.

Almost an hour passed as the newspaper finally collapsed in Holmes' lap. He had read most of the articles but needed to make a change. "Watson, the dining car beckons." He stood up while folding the newspaper and tucking it under his arm.

The mother was sitting next to Watson, and she gave a look of apology. "I'm so sorry, sir. This is the children's first train trip. I had told my husband I thought we should have reserved an entire compartment. But by the time he had purchased the tickets, there were no compartments available." Holmes responded with a weak smile as he reached to get his hat from the rack overhead.

"Coming, Watson? Holmes asked with exasperation in his voice.

Holmes led the way through the four-passenger cars to reach the dining area. Tables were being cleared from breakfast, and only a few diners remained. Holmes walked back to the last table at the end of the car as the waiter was laying a fresh white tablecloth.

"I think this will do nicely, Watson." Holmes sat facing the window, which showed the open countryside, with green fields and livestock passing by. When the server came to the table, Holmes said to him, "Bring me Earl Grey tea and scones."

"Yes, sir. I'll place your order immediately. And you?" he said to Watson. The waiter left when Watson shook his head.

"You didn't get enough scones at the hotel?" Watson asked, chuckling.

"I can't have tea without scones; it wouldn't be proper. Besides, I have no intention of going back to the compartment until it's time to retrieve our baggage."

"But that's at least ten hours," Watson said.

"Precisely."

"Well, in that case, I'm going back to retrieve a book from my suitcase. Can I bring back anything for you?"

"No, thank you, Watson."

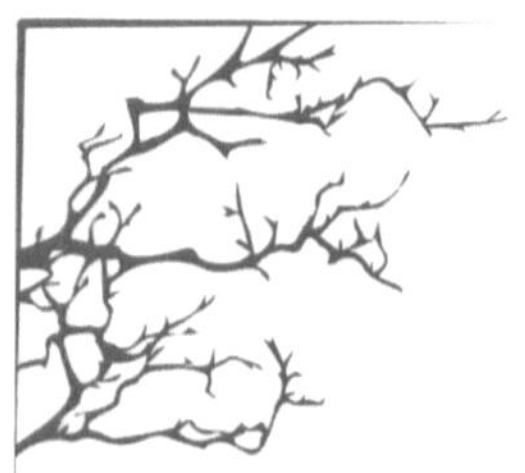

Chapter Eleven

Once the train arrived in London, Sherlock Holmes hailed a carriage parked just beyond the platform. He planned to take him and Dr. Watson to Scotland Yard directly. With Inspector Lestrade's words of urgency whispering in his ear, Holmes told Watson that they needed to meet with the Inspector immediately, despite the late hour.

The carriage deposited them at the front steps of the police station. A lone Bobbie stood just past the entrance, smoking a cigarette, the dim lighting casting dark shadows on his face.

They entered through the stone archway and a pair of double doors, in desperate need of painting. Then Holmes and Watson walked to the long reception counter and were met by the night desk officer.

The officer sized up the two men standing before him, "What can I do for you, gentlemen, at this time of night." The officer smiled at them conspiratorially, "Don't tell me... you got your pockets picked while out on the town over on the east side?" he chuckled under his breath.

Holmes put out his hand, "If you only stop speculating, we can get on with our business." The officer scowled at Holmes' rebuke. "We have come to speak with Inspector Lestrade. He is expecting us."

The officer leaned over the counter, and his garlic breath was almost too overpowering. "You won't be able to see the Inspector. He is not here," the officer said with finality.

"Where is he?" Holmes said, now irritated with the desk clerk. "Lestrade asked us to meet him here when we returned to London."

The desk officer looked at a note posted behind the counter. "Are you Sherlock Holmes?"

"Yes," he said, starting to lose his patience.

"Wait here, and I'll get Inspector Grayson. He can answer your questions." The desk sergeant left them to wait.

Within a few minutes, a young man, overly dressed for his position, ushered Holmes and Watson into an interrogation room. "Please take a seat," he directed as he pulled on his gold cuff-linked sleeves. "My name is Inspector Grayson. I understand Inspector Lestrade was expecting you and is soliciting your assistance on a particular case."

"Inspector, it's late. We've been on a train all day and don't have time for your foolishness. If you have a message from Lestrade, then give it to us. Otherwise, we will be on our way."

The detective was not used to having someone speak to him in this manner. "I don't know who you are or why Inspector Lestrade would take you into his confidence, but he apparently has." The edge to his voice was sharp.

"If you have something to tell us, then do so. Otherwise, I have a soft bed waiting." Holmes moved his chair back, preparing to stand up and leave.

Grayson weighed his limited options before saying, "Earlier this evening, Inspector Lestrade received injuries while in pursuit of a criminal. A passing wagon struck him and knocked him to the ground, hitting his head on the cobblestone. Let me assure you; he'll be fine. But they took him to Guys Hospital as a precaution." Holmes could tell the Inspector was bristling about what he would say next. "Inspector Lestrade is working on a case that they had also assigned to me. Though I'm afraid I have to disagree with his assessment."

Watson watched as Holmes' fingers drummed on the tabletop. Holmes said, "Perhaps you could give me the details."

Inspector Grayson began pacing the room like a caged lion. He felt trapped by the circumstances and begrudged telling this stranger anything about the case. Unable to put it off any longer, he saw Holmes pushing his chair back further.

"It started about a year ago when a series of mysterious deaths occurred. Most I felt were nothing more than unlucky accidents. However, later, a few cases appeared to be connected. But of course, this is a considerable-sized metropolitan and not without its criminal elements," the Inspector said defensively.

"Inspector Lestrade felt the common link was the fact that these particular murders, as he calls them, were each committed on the first day of each month." Grayson stopped pacing the room. "They assigned me to the case after a reported death that occurred on January-one of this year. In truth, I still question whether this was a murder or a terrible accident and lean towards the second. In any event, on the first day of each proceeding month, there has been a suspicious death. I have found no reason to believe these occurrences have any connections. But, after a reported death on September 1, they brought in Inspector Lestrade to assist me with the unsolved cases. Since then, three more murders have occurred on the first of each month. There, there is no question. The victims were most unquestionably murdered."

Holmes raised his hand to stop the Inspector's words from proceeding and told the Inspector, "I'll need the reports for each death."

Grayson glared at Holmes, "That could be a problem." He fidgeted with his jacket.

"And why is that," Holmes asked, irritated with this upstart of a detective.

"Well, I have all the detailed reports on the first nine cases in my possession, but I haven't been able to locate the last three murder files from Inspector Lestrade's."

Holmes sighed with disdain, "Gather what you have, and I'll take them with me," he said.

"What?" the Inspector shouted. "You expect me to release police reports to a civilian?" Grayson stammered.

"You don't think I'll sit here and review the files at this table with you watching over my shoulder, do you?" Sherlock Holmes stood. "Perhaps we should speak with the Chief Inspector."

They quickly resolved the impasse with the mention of the Chief Inspector. "Wait here while I go to my desk and get you the copies of my cases." Grayson left the room, chastened.

"What do you think, Holmes?" Watson asked.

"I think this young detective is in over his head, and they brought in Lestrade to solve a serial murder case."

Watson slowly shook his head. "You pack people into buildings like they're canned sardines, and this is what you get. I read somewhere in The Times we're nearing five million residents in this metro area population. Where is the clean living in that? Most people don't have the means."

"Let's not jump to conclusions just yet," Holmes said.

Minutes later, Inspector Grayson entered with an armload of folders and laid them on the desk in front of Sherlock Holmes. "These are what I have, and here is a list of names in total that Lestrade wanted you to take a look at. He said something about how you could make connections where everyone else saw nothing, but I don't see how that is possible."

Holmes raised his eyebrows as he read the names and dates of the victims. "Keep looking for Lestrade's cases. I'll take these for now, and you can send the others when you find them or when Lestrade can tell you where they are." Sherlock Holmes gathered the files in his arms. "Watson, we're done here," he said as he led Watson out of the interrogation room and left the Inspector dumbfounded.

Outside, the carriage was still waiting, with the driver leaning against the building, smoking a cigarette. "Bout time you come out. Would've gone in meself to look fer you if I wasn't keepin an eye on yur luggage." The driver tossed his half-smoked cigarette into the gutter. "Me misses is gona be mad how late I am coming home." He said this, hoping to receive a larger gratuity.

It was now after midnight before Holmes and Dr. Watson walked through the door at two-twenty-one B Baker Street. The driver made several trips up the stairs with baggage and was well rewarded for his service.

"I know better than to ask if you are retiring for the evening. But I'm going to bed and sleep for a week," Watson said in parting.

"Good night, Watson. I'll ask Mrs. Hudson to prepare a decent breakfast when you wake." Holmes turned his attention to building a fire in the sitting room.

With Watson tucked away for the night, Holmes changed into his dressing robe to sit by the fire so he could start with the files.

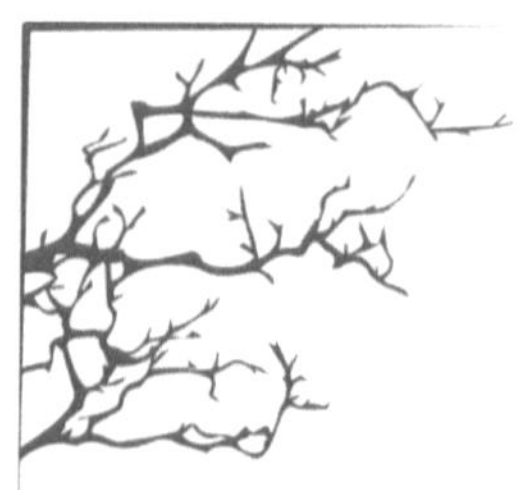

Chapter Twelve

Sherlock Holmes stoked the fire until it blazed and filled the room with its dancing brilliance. He poured a small brandy and settled into his wing chair with the first file dated January first.

It read that Bartholomew Ludkin, a chimney sweeper, age thirty-four and single, was found hanging from a rope tied off to the stonework at a site presumed to be where he was cleaning a flue. The body was sighted by a neighbor before the predawn hour from her kitchen window on Canonbury Place on the morning of January second.

No sign of foul play was reported by the Constable called to the scene. The body was removed and sent to the coroner for an inspection. His report stated the body had mysterious bruises on his arms but noted these could all be part of work-related injuries considering the hazards of the trade.

They registered death as asphyxiation. Holmes understood that meant the neck did not break with the fall, and he probably hung there for several minutes, struggling to free himself. The coroner ruled the case as an accident with questionable characteristics without other evidence.

Sherlock Holmes made a note to view the building and the location of the chimney in relation to where they found the body hanging. Several questions arose: What was the sweep's work habit? Did he often work after sunset? Where was his wagon or equipment at the site?

Inspector Grayson's report lacked these details. Once the coroner had given his official opinion, the Inspector did not proceed further with the investigation.

Holmes closed the folder, placed it on the floor by his feet, and picked up the February first file.

James Thatcher, gardener, age fifty-seven, was found floating face down in a garden fountain at Fountain Cottage off The Grove. His body was not discovered until February fifth because of the unusual winter snow.

The autopsy report said Mr. Thatcher drowned with evidence of water in his lungs. The report also showed clear evidence of trauma to the head but stopped short of saying by blunt force. James Thatcher was single and lived on the grounds in a small hut provided to him by the property owner. Those interviewed said he often did not see the gardener on a daily basis because of the size of the property, and the gardener tended to keep to himself.

Inspector Grayson had asked if he had seen any unusual activity or seen anyone on the property since the day of the gardener's death.

The person who discovered the body, William Bond, said he had been curious why the garbage hadn't been removed. It was one of the additional tasks of the gardener. He said he was on his way to the gardener's hut that sat at the far end of the property and passed within fifty feet of the fountain when he spotted what turned out to be a leg covered in snow hanging on the edge of the stonework. Mr. Bond went to investigate and saw what had happened. He further stated that he noticed more than one set of footprints in the snow because it had a frozen, crusted layer that kept the imprints intact. He told the Inspector that James Thatcher had very large feet for his height, and there was a set of smaller tracks mixed with those of Thatcher's.

Grayson made a notation, dismissing the connection, thinking the prints could have already been there before the accident.

Inspector Grayson could find no reason for anyone wanting to harm James Thatcher and therefore concluded this was an accidental death.

Sherlock Holmes poked the fire while thinking these first two cases were far from settled. He took his pipe off the stand and had one last smoke before retiring for the night.

THE SUN WAS UP AND peeking through Watson's drapes as he opened his eyes. Between their adventure in Bristol and a trip overseas trip to America, Watson was happy to be back in his bed. He could hear Holmes moving around in the kitchen, taking plates off the shelf and closing cabinet doors with a bang. This was a trick Holmes used to get Watson up and dressed. He rose and slipped on his robe and slippers, then sought out Holmes in the kitchen.

"I'm sorry, Holmes. Did I sleep too late?" Watson asked while still tying off his robe.

"No, no, not at all, my dear Watson. Mrs. Hudson just left a few moments ago. She has brought us a hearty breakfast." Watson stretched his arms out and yawned as he entered the kitchen. "Sit down, and I'll dish you up a plate."

Holmes uncovered a tray and filled Watson's plate with back bacon, eggs, sausage, baked beans, a few fried tomatoes, sauteed mushrooms, and two slices of toasted bread. "I know you prefer coffee, and it's about ready." Watson tucked a cloth napkin under his chin and attacked the food like he hadn't eaten in a week.

Holmes poured coffee into a cup, asking, "Milk, Watson?"

"No, thank you. You know I never add milk, but you never stop trying to convert me," Watson said, slightly garbled with a mouthful of baked beans.

Holmes's plate was a bit lighter than Watson's. And he would stay with his preferred Earl Grey tea.

"I hope you didn't stay up all night going over the cases," Watson said. "By the time my head hit the pillow, I was fast asleep and slept the sleep of the dead."

"No, I examined only the first two files. Inspector Grayson attributes accidental death in both cases. But I find his judgment incomplete. Later today, I think I'll want to see the sites myself before making a conclusion. Even though a year has passed, some clues may still be evident.

"Do you care for some company, or would you prefer a solo trip? It looks like we might have a sunny day. And I'm feeling refreshed with proper rest."

"Watson, I always enjoy your input on a case and would be delighted for the company," Holmes said with a smile.

As Watson ate his breakfast, Holmes made his tea and ate from his more meager portions while reading the Times.

Watson finished first and removed his plate from the table. "I'll get dressed for travel and be ready when you are, Holmes." Watson left with Sherlock Holmes' face still buried in the paper.

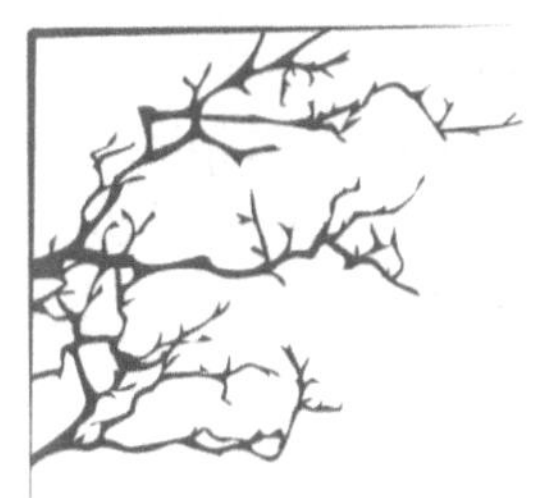

Chapter Thirteen

While Dr. Watson finished the last touches to his attire, Sherlock Holmes dashed down to the street to hail a carriage for the day.

When Watson came out of his room, he noticed his friend was already downstairs. He exited the apartment wrapped in his winter Grey wool long coat and bowler hat. His hands gloved with the leather gloves he had purchased in New York.

"A lovely day, wouldn't you agree, Holmes?" Watson said as he approached his friend standing curbside. Holmes was waving at a coach coming up the street.

"The Paper says it will rain by this afternoon, but since when are they ever right?" Holmes replied jovially.

The cab driver waited for his fares to board, "Where to," the coachman asked Holmes as he and Watson settled into the carriage.

"Canonbury House off Upper Street," Holmes said.

"Yes, yes, I know the area. It's just beyond Canonbury Square. Sit back, and I'll get you there straight away, sir." The driver closed the carriage door and mounted to his coachman's seat.

The sun's warmth made the ride to their destination pleasant. With light traffic and few pedestrians, the ride ended all too soon for Watson. Bright, crisp winter days like this were rare. Even the air felt clean, scrubbed by the early morning breeze.

Holmes stepped out of the cab at their first destination and began filling his pipe. "Coming, Watson?" Homes asked. He lifted his head to the driver and said, "I don't know how long this will take."

"No trouble, sir. I have a Dickens novel to read and am used to long waits. You take all the time you need, and I'll be here with old man Scrooge." The driver pulled a red wool blanket from under his seat and covered his legs.

Sherlock Holmes walked along Canonbury Place on the opposite side of the street from where the neighbor reported the body. He stood silent, pipe still unlit, and looked up at the roof of the building from which the sweep had died. Holmes struck a match and lit his pipe, drawing in quick puffs. "Watson, what do you see on the rooftop?"

Watson knew from his manner of speech that Holmes asked a forensic question. "A slate roof, perhaps at a three-degree angle. There is little sign of moss growth and only traces in the shaded area away from the chimney. Several small vent pipes and the brick chimney were constructed a third of the way in on the east side."

"Very good. How is it that an experienced chimney sweep should find himself hanging over the edge that far from the chimney he was working on?" Holmes pointed to where the body had been found hanging.

"He could have had his ladder at that end of the building, but that makes no sense. The roof angle is slight and much easier to approach from a lower height," Watson answered.

"Precisely," Sherlock Holmes smiled at his associate, "I'll make a detective of you yet, Watson." Holmes declared, "Bartholomew Ludkin is a victim of murder."

Holmes crossed the street to examine the grounds around the building. He'd stop to view the roof line in several areas. "I think we can move on to the next location." With that pronouncement, Holmes headed back to the carriage.

The carriage ride took much longer. Canonbury Road was on the city's north edge, and their next destination was almost at the opposite end of London. The metropolis was fully awake at midday with all its noise and lively activity. Holmes seemed indifferent to it, but Watson truly loved living in the heart of a grand metropolitan even after his tirade the night before. "Holmes, perhaps we can stop for lunch on the Strand after viewing the last site?"

"I'm surprised you would even think of food after the meal Mrs. Hudson provided this morning," Holmes said with a faint grin.

"I know you too well, Holmes. If we go back to the apartment, you will hold up in your chair and chew on these cases until you have worked out every detail. It's too nice of a day to be sitting behind closed doors."

"Alright, Watson. Perhaps tea and toast would be agreeable after we're concluded."

The carriage pulled over on The Grove, fronting Fountain Cottage. All the trees were devoid of leaves, giving an open view of the grounds. The substantial fountain dominated the foreground, with the cottage sited furthest back from the street. Though the house is described as a cottage, it was five-hundred and fifty square meters spread across the estate.

Sherlock Holmes left the paved pathway and led Watson to the water feature. Its base rose above their knees and was reasonably distant from the house. "I want to have a word with whoever resides here," he said as Holmes crossed the lawn, kicking through a layer of dry-brown leaves. Apparently, the new gardener hadn't yet attended to them.

The two-story brick cottage had many windows facing the fountain on both levels and a single, sparse row of trees with branches missing their covers. Holmes stood on the stoop and looked back at the water feature. He could clearly see it and the surrounding paths. "Hard to imagine anyone not seeing what happened." Sherlock Holmes knocked on the door and waited almost a minute before footfalls declared a coming answer.

An older man with white hair and bent back unlatched the door. "What can I do for you," he asked, not gruff but not friendly either.

"My name is Sherlock Holmes, and this is Dr. Watson, my associate. We've come to ask a few questions concerning the death of your gardener last February."

"He wasn't my gardener. I'm just the house caretaker. But that's neither here nor there, is it?"

"No. But I would appreciate speaking with anyone who might have witnessed anything that day."

"There was only me. The owners spend their winters in Sicily. They leave in early October and return in April. I take care of the property while they're gone."

"Did you see him near the fountain on the day of his death? Or is there any reason to believe he died nefariously?"

"Neither. Part of my job is to keep watch for trespassers. And that would be primarily children. They think a fountain is a playground. But it had snowed all during that day and obscured my vision. It was also quite cold, I remember. At least the parents were sensible enough to keep their children indoors."

The man continued, "Now, we do get people strolling the pathways quite often. As long as they stay off the grass, I don't have a problem with that."

"Were there strollers last winter?"

"Sometimes. I did notice, however, one particular older couple. I'd never seen them before. I thought it odd; they walked the paths for six days in a row. Then, I have not seen the couple since the accident. Perhaps the idea of someone dying in the fountain made them choose another route."

"Can you give me a description," Holmes asked.

The caretaker chuckled. "I'm almost seventy, and my eyes aren't that good. But I'll tell you what I can. It looked to me like they were dressed in wealthy gentlemen's and gentle ladies' attire. Both may be mid-fifties and very much in love. I reasoned that by how she clung to her partner."

"Is there anything else you might add," Holmes said.

"Sorry. I liked James; he took beautiful care of the grounds and treated them like his own property. Not like the bloke we have now. The worthless sot."

"Watson, we're finished here," Holmes said. Holmes turned back to the caretaker and said, "My condolences."

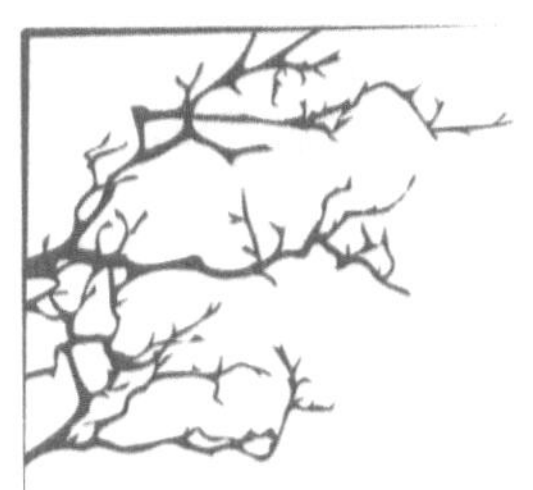

Chapter Fourteen

Sherlock Holmes built an afternoon fire and slipped into his comfortable smoking jacket. Seated in his chair and feet upon the ottoman, Watson brought Holmes a sniffer of brandy. "I assume you're about to read through more case files. So, I thought you might like a drink to sip on while reading."

"Thank you, Watson. What are you planning for this afternoon?"

"I thought I would review and consolidate my notes from our case in Bristol. The paper is hoping to print the story in a few days." Sherlock Holmes sighed at the thought.

The March folder lay open in Holmes' lap as he read. Andrew Becket, a retired Naval Officer, age sixty-seven, was found in the wooded section of Westbourne Park. Mr. and Mrs. Peterson of Blackman Lane discovered his body while taking their evening constitution. They told the police that they had almost missed seeing the body because it was twilight and the shadows were dark in the woods.

The first Constable on the scene reported the body was partially behind a tree but with one leg snagged in the crook of a tree root. Andrew Becket's head has a single gash, approximately three and one-half inches, running from an inch above his left eyebrow to halfway down his cheek. The Constable reported there appeared to be no signs of a struggle but also said the old leaves were thick and could find no footprints of either the victim or if there was an assailant. He saw blood at the base of the tree and concluded Mr. Becket must have had an imminent need to relieve himself. Therefore, he most likely tripped over the root and hit his head on the tree trunk. He passed this opinion along to the coroner, and they decided no autopsy was needed.

Inspector Grayson reviewed the file and signed off on it as accidental death on March fifth and filed the report as such.

Sherlock Holmes made some mental notes and finished the brandy. He reached for his pipe and added the shag tobacco but discovered an empty matchbox. Rising out of his comfortable chair, Holmes looked for matches on the mantle where he drew one out and lit it on the firebox before having a smoke. He paced the room and looked out the window twice to clear his mind. He glanced over at Watson, who was deeply ingrained with his writing.

"Still at it, Watson?"

"I'm putting it to paper as we speak." Holmes looked glumly at Watson and returned to his chair.

The April file was just as thin as the other files. Holmes wondered if Inspector Grayson was incapable of identifying a murder, even if it took place right in front of him with a smoking gun held in the killer's hand.

Holmes opened the folder and let out a rush of air, expecting the worse. It started with the victim's name, Philip Chatsworth, a laborer employed at The Four Mills, age thirty-two, and married. They found the body when the morning shift crew came to work the next day. They reported a Miss. Sanderson had nearly slipped to the floor in a viscous liquid. She realized it was blood and screamed, bringing the other workers to her location. The manager was notified, and the police came shortly after that.

It took several hours to disassemble the machinery and remove the body's remaining. The unusual wedding ring he wore, and the flannel cap identified Mr. Chadsworth, found near the machinery area. This was the first fatality at the mill in seven years. And the night foreman told the police he had seen Philip twenty minutes before quitting time, down on the main floor, oiling the gears.

Once more, Inspector Grayson quickly labeled this an industrial accident and closed the case. The interviews conducted by the Inspector were cursory at best.

"I'm finished," Watson said as he laid the pen on top of the papers. "I'll take the story down to the newspaper first thing in the morning."

Sherlock Holmes put the folder in his hand on the table, wishing he had never agreed to let Watson memorialize his adventures. After two years, strangers were approaching him in recognition, which went against his desire for anonymity. Holmes couldn't care less if anyone knew of his part in solving Scotland Yard cases. But Holmes understood Watson's indignation at the Yard's willingness to take undue credit. Watson felt it was unfair to Holmes. He had said so on many occasions.

Sherlock Holmes sprang from his chair, "Watson, Let's go to dinner. I hear there is a new café that just opened on Clay Street, and its specialty is a calzone baked in a brick oven."

"Holmes, you amaze me. How is it you know these things?" said I.

"Elementary, Watson. I walked by the café a week before we left for Bristol. And I peered into the window, watching them install the new oven. The owner came out and told me the date of their opening. There's no mystery to that, Watson," Holmes said with a laugh.

Holmes and Watson turned onto Dorset Street as the twilight was dwindling, and the lamplighters were igniting the streetlights. How soon would this scene change? Holmes had given no thought to how his mission would alter the lives of these men. But progress always has a price.

Within a few short blocks, they turned into the small side street where the café sign hung over the door. Three people stood outside the door waiting, and Holmes and Watson joined them. It took ten minutes before a couple of tables cleared, and those waiting outside could enter.

Antonio's was the first Italian restaurant to open in London. The family had emigrated two years earlier and saved every shilling since to make their dream possible.

Holmes opened the door to come inside and near bowled over by noise from the packed establishment. It was hot and smokey. The rich aroma of Italian spices was so strong that one could taste it on their lips, and they both felt like they'd died and gone to heaven.

Both ordered the recommended calzone, though neither had ever tasted it before. The server came and set a Ricasoli Vineyard's Chianti bottle at the table. Holmes and Watson ate every scrap when the meal was presented and nearly finished the bottle.

"My God, Holmes. I do believe we need to travel more for our own sake. What else are we missing out there?" Watson said while sipping his wine. He held the glass up to view it closer, saying the only Italian word he knew, "Bella, Bella." Holmes smiled at Watson's English dialect.

After dinner, they extended the walk by going over to Gloucester Street, traveling down to Berkeley, and completing the loop back up Baker. Mrs. Hudson was at the bottom of the landing when the men came home. "Good evening, Mr. Holmes. Good evening, Dr. Watson. Did you go out for a meal? I have steak and kidney pie leftover if you haven't."

Watson said, "Thank you, Mrs. Hudson. We did indeed go out. We had our first Italian dinner, and it was marvelous."

Mrs. Hudson shook her head, "There's nothing wrong with proper English food. First the French; now Italian. What's next? Chinese," she continued to shake her head as she hurried back into her apartment.

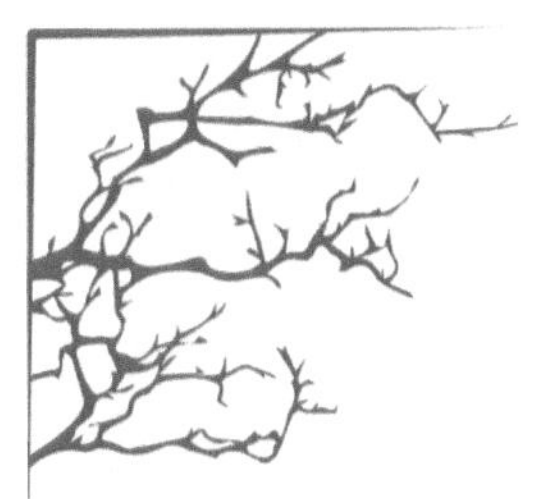

Chapter Fifteen

Though the Italian dinner left Holmes feeling sleepy, he sat back in his wing chair and took out the fifth folder.

Thaddaeus Broadwick, age eighty-four, was a small shop owner on the corner of Union and Cross Street. The Clock Works was run solely by Mr. Broadwick with no employees. On the night of May first, a concerned tenant occupying the business directly across the street noticed Thaddaeus's lights were still lit after ten pm. He knew Mr. Broadwick never worked past five.

The witness, David Becker, flagged the Constable walking his beat on Union Street. Mr. Becker told the officer of his concern that something was amiss with the old man. Together, they crossed the street and knocked on Mr. Broadwick's door. When no answer came, they tried the knob and found it unlocked. Once inside, they found the back shop had been ransacked. Most of the wall clocks were now in broken piles strewn across the floor, and Thaddaeus Broadwick's body lay face down behind the workbench. They ascertained the owner was indeed dead.

Inspector Grayson arrived an hour later to investigate. Grayson wrote I examined the body by first turning it over and discovering the cause of death. The victim had a large gold pocket watch stuffed into his mouth. It is my assumption this was a robbery, and the timepiece was used to keep the victim from calling out. In his report, the coroner confirmed my hypothesis that the victim suffocated, taking at least a half-hour to do so.

It is unclear what the thief took, and to date, no wares have appeared in pawnshops.

Sherlock Holmes slammed the file closed, not bothering to read more. It took a lot to get Holmes' ire up, and incompetence on this scale was one of them. Holmes felt suddenly tired and decided to read the other reports when he was fresh.

The fire was already down to embers, and Holmes extinguished the lights before retiring for the night.

DR. WATSON ROSE WITH the first rays of the sun. He listened for familiar noises in the apartment but heard none. "Holmes?" Watson called. There was no response. He left his room and called again. "Holmes, where are you?" Watson looked from room to room. He ended up in the kitchen and saw the wrinkled paper on the square table. Holmes' teacup sat empty in the saucer with a soiled spoon. There was no note, but since when did Holmes ever give that courtesy? Watson put water on to boil and settled in with the morning newspaper.

SHERLOCK HOLMES HIRED a carriage to take him to his first stop, Westbourne Park. Westbourne Park drew many visitors, even during the winter. But while it wasn't raining, the cloud cover and stiff breeze kept all but the hardiest walkers home.

Holmes followed the directions in the report to the exact location where the body had been found. He didn't expect to glean any hard evidence after this long, but the site could tell him something about the event. He located the tree with the protruding root six feet off the trail. What wasn't in the report was a tree a few feet past this spot and at the walkway's edge. Holmes examined the tree and determined a person could easily remain hidden behind it.

Then, Sherlock Holmes walked around the tree where the body had been. The report stated that Andrew Becket's head had hit a knot on the trunk that caused the terrible gash, and though there was no coroner's report, one had to assume the skull would have been fractured in order to cause death.

As Holmes stood off to the side, he calculated the length from the protruding root to the knot. Andrew Becket was five-ten, almost three inches too short of having his foot snagged in the root, and still made contact with the knot at the contact point on his forehead.

Holmes saw everything he needed to and walked back to the waiting carriage. "Do you know where the Four Mills is located?" Holmes asked.

"Yes, sir. I've got a cousin that works out there. He says it's not a bad place to be."

The carriage pulled up to a series of identical buildings, and Sherlock Holmes asked a laborer where he might find the manager's office. In a strong cockney accent, the man spoke, "Last building," he pointed, "go through the lobby, and he's on the second floor."

With that, the carriage moved down the street and stopped in front of the designated entry. Holmes told the driver that this could take some time. "No worries, I've got me lunch right here." The driver lifted a soiled burlap bag to show him.

The manager's office had a second-floor wall of windows overlooking the massive machine works. Sherlock Holmes came through the lobby door and was greeted by a middle-aged man in a white shop coat. "How can I help you, sir?" he said as he emerged from behind a receptionist's counter.

Holmes said, "I need to speak with the plant manager, Mr. Ash. My name is Sherlock Holmes."

"Do you have an appointment? Mr. Ash is a very busy man." The man looked closer at Holmes, realizing he was speaking with a gentleman. "In what regards is your request?"

"I'm here to investigate the death of Philip Chatsworth."

"I don't understand why you're here. The police determined Mr. Chatsworth's death was accidental, and you certainly are not from the insurance company. We have long since settled with Mrs. Chatsworth. And she is receiving a reasonable pension, even though her husband was many years from retirement. Are you an attorney?" the man started to look suspiciously at Holmes.

"Scotland Yard may have been rash in closing this case. That is why I need to speak with the manager."

"Please wait here. I'll let Mr. Ash know of your concerns." The man left Holmes and slipped through an office door.

Fredrick Ash was tall, broad-shouldered, and a born salesman. He came through the door with a beaming smile, and his hand extended like he was greeting an old friend. "Welcome, Mr. Holmes. How may I be of assistance? Theo says you're here to investigate poor Mr. Chatsworth's death, a sorry affair. He was an exceptional employee and respected by his co-workers."

"Yes, I'm sure," Holmes cut him off. "I want to speak with Miss Sanderson and the foreman who were there when the body was discovered."

Mr. Ash turned his head toward Theo and said, "Theo, will you go down to the main floor and locate Miss Sanderson? She should still be at her station. Then ask Teddy to join us at the accident site." He said, "Teddy is the shop work supervisor, turning back to Holmes. Top-notch." Pointing back to the door, Sherlock Holmes came through. Ash led the way out to the corridor and down the interior stairway.

As the two men came to the site, the assistant ushered Miss Sanderson over. "Wilma, this is Mr. Holmes," Ash said. Mr. Ash smiled at Sherlock Holmes, saying, "I make it a point to know all our employees by their first names. We're a family here," turning back to Miss Sanderson. "Aren't we, Wilma?"

Holmes detected a warning in his tone of voice. "Mr. Ash, I would speak in private with Miss Sanderson if you please."

Fredrick Ash was not pleased. He frowned at Holmes, but he and the two other men moved to the far end. Holmes walked with Miss. Sanderson over to the location of the machinery. "Please tell me exactly what you saw on the morning of Mr. Chadsworth's death."

Miss Sanderson's eyes welled with tears. Sherlock Holmes took out his handkerchief and gave it to her. "My shift starts at six a.m., and I was walking to my station over there," she pointed to the machine she operated. "I'm usually the first person on the station because of the sequence of operation. And well..." she began to sob.

"I understand how difficult this is, Miss Sanderson. Please take your time," Holmes encouraged.

"The blood... I slipped in a pool of blood. What a horrible way to die."

Holmes wanted her to focus, "Please describe what you saw."

Miss. Sanderson took a deep breath before continuing, "A stream of blood ran from the press, and I could see the fabric of his coat still visible, and poor

Mr. Chadsworth's cap was lying on the floor." She dabbed at her eyes with the kerchief.

"Thank you, Miss Sanderson. You have been a great help," Holmes said.

"Is that it?" she asked, wondering what she said that made Sherlock Holmes end the conversation.

Sherlock Holmes waved to the waiting men. As they came back, Holmes said, "Now I will speak with you," Holmes pointed to the supervisor.

"Teddy Lawson, sir," the work supervisor said.

"I understand you were the last to see Mr. Chadsworth alive?"

"Yes, sir. The evening shift was about to clock out, and Philip was finishing his duties. I waved to him from over there," he pointed where he had been just standing. "I said good night and left the floor through that door," he indicated to a door in the corner of the wall.

"You were here when the body was exhumed from the machinery, yes?"

"Yes. I'll never be free from that awful sight."

"The police report says Mr. Chadsworth had his overcoat on at the time of his death. Is this common?"

"Oh, no, sir. In fact, it's strictly forbidden for this very reason. Loose clothing is dangerous around these machines."

"Was Mr. Chadsworth wearing his coat the last time you saw him?"

Teddy Lawson thought about that question for a moment. "Well, no."

"Thank you, Mr. Lawson," Holmes said. "I'm almost finished here. Mr. Ash, it appears your building has other trades and deliveries coming in and out of this facility. Is that correct?"

"Why, yes, Mr. Holmes. It would be complicated to operate otherwise."

"That's all the questions I have," Holmes said. "I can find my way out." He left them still pondering what had just taken place.

Chapter Sixteen

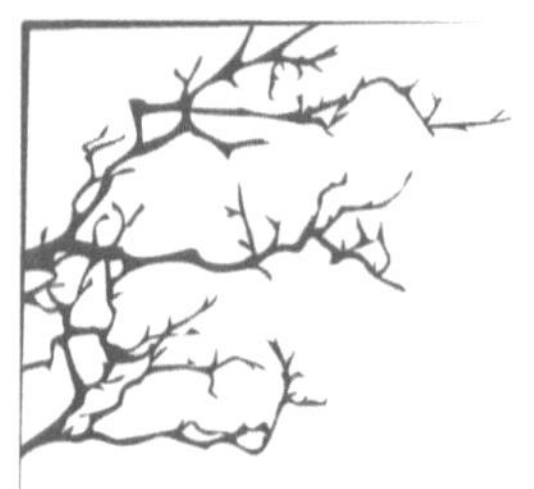

Sherlock Holmes directed the carriage driver to the corner of Cross and Union Street. At this time of day, the streets were packed with activity, and the walkways were crowded. Holmes sat in the carriage, looking at the closed and quiet shop on the corner. The Clock shop still had its wares displayed, though the store remained closed. He viewed the shop across the road from where the report originated and saw a middle-aged man looking out the window.

Holmes exited the carriage, waited for an opening in the traffic, and crossed over. He looked up at the storefront sign with a black grand piano painted on a white background. Holmes opened the door, and a bell jingled from overhead. The shopkeeper left the front window and came to greet him, "Welcome," he said with a smile. "Have you come for our sale this week?"

"No," Holmes said, "I have a few questions about Mr. Broadwick's death."

"You're from Scotland Yard?"

"I'm an investigator. The file said you alerted the police and had been concerned something was amiss at the clock shop."

"Oh yes, Thaddaeus' habits were like clockwork," David Becker caught himself. Sorry, that was a terrible pun. He never altered his routine, and I became concerned when I noticed his lights on. He was an old man and could have had a medical emergency. The shop owners around here try to keep watch for each other. We tend to get more than our share of sticky fingers if you know what I mean."

Holmes asked, "Why were you here at that hour?"

"I have an apartment in the back of the store. The only window looks out at a brick wall in the alley. Sometimes, I like to stand here and watch. You'd be surprised by how busy this street can be, even at night."

"You don't get a lot of business," Holmes said.

"Don't need much. One sale takes care of my overhead for six months."

"So, it is common for you to be doing what you were doing when I came in?"

"As I said, yes."

"Tell me if you can recall any patrons who might have visited the clock shop frequently?"

"Odd that you would ask that. I did notice a woman, quite attractive, I might say. She came a few times and later brought a gentleman who appeared to be a cripple. The man returned several other times without her." Mr. Becker hesitated a moment, "Sometimes people have the most challenging time in choosing their purchase," he added.

"When was the last time you saw this gentleman go into the shop?"

"Well, come to think of it, earlier on the day of the robbery. He'd been there, I'd say, around noon, but I haven't seen him since."

Sherlock Holmes turned towards the door and opened it. "Thank you for your assistance, good day." Holmes dashed back across the street, immediately climbed back into the carriage, and told the driver to bring him back to Baker Street.

Upon his return, Holmes climbed the stairs two at a time and was met by Watson at the door. "There you are, Holmes. I asked Mrs. Hudson if she would make lunch for us. I've already eaten, but there is food on the table if you desire."

Holmes put on the teakettle and ate the sandwich Mrs. Hudson had made for him while standing by the stove. After pouring his tea, he took it to his fireplace chair and resumed reading the police files.

Judas Goldman, age fifty-seven, was found in his home on June third. There were no signs of forced entry. On inspection, all the windows were securely locked. Both front and back doors are also secured. The house cleaner discovered his body. When asked, she told Scotland Yard that she had left the house two days before after a thorough cleaning. Mr. Goldman's occupation was as a music teacher and violin tutor.

Inspector Grayson could clearly see the cause of death. They strangled the victim with a violin G-string. After inspecting the home, Inspector Grayson could not conclude the motive for the murder. It appeared they left the house undisturbed.

Sherlock Holmes looked at the address of Mr. Goldman's residence. It was a small house on Camberwell Road, just north of Camberwell Green.

Holmes literally jumped out of his chair, rushed over to his library cabinet, and sorted through the shelves. He pulled out a long paper roll and a small box. He walked over to the fireplace, removed a picture from the wall, and unrolled a London city map, hanging it in place of the oil painting.

Holmes took the files, starting with the first, and he pushed in a straight pin at each location. A pattern was beginning to develop. Holmes opened the next folder, looking only for the crime site. The nine files came into view, and the three remaining files that Inspector Lestrade had would complete the picture.

Watson had said something about going out shopping for a Christmas gift for Mrs. Hudson and not to expect him before dinner. Holmes looked at the calendar lying on his desk. Today was December twenty-second.

Injured or not, Sherlock Holmes needed to see Inspector Lestrade. He threw on his coat and hailed a hansom. "Guy's Hospital," he said, climbing into his seat.

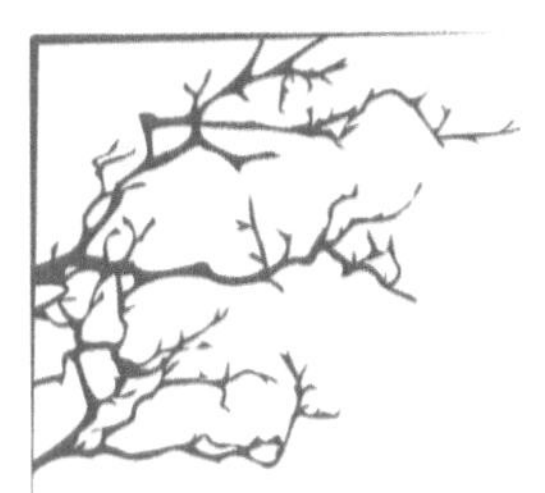

Chapter Seventeen

Sherlock Holmes arrived at Guy's Hospital and, while paying the driver, told him he wouldn't need his services. Following an orderly pushing a patient through the entry door in a wheelchair, Holmes entered the hospital's main entrance.

The lobby reminded him of King's Cross railway station just after a train arrival. He stood in the entry for a moment to get his bearings. Like the parting of the Red Sea, the flow of humanity opened to reveal the reception desk. He crossed the lobby and stood for several minutes at the counter, waiting for the desk nurse to finish her conversation with a doctor. When the nurse had finished, she looked up at Holmes with a tired expression.

"My name is Sherlock Holmes, and I'd like to know which room Inspector Lestrade is staying in."

The nurse's eyes narrowed at Holmes, "Are you from Scotland Yard?" she asked officiously.

"I am an associate of Lestrade's. He wired me from Liverpool to see him as soon as possible. My understanding is that it's urgent." Holmes's voice sharpened.

The woman leaned over the low counter in front of her and picked up a chart. She scanned the list, running her finger down the page. "Yes, here he is," she paused. "Room two-seventeen, but I'm afraid you can't see him now." The nurse looked up, expecting the man to acquiesce. Holmes continued to look at her. She huffed, "He's in therapy for the next hour or so."

Sherlock Holmes moved away from the reception desk and headed towards the stairs without further discussion. He could hear the nurse admonishing him not to go up to the second floor, but Holmes ignored her.

Room two-seventeen was indeed empty, with a bed wrinkled from use. Holmes decided to wait in the room for Lestrade's return rather than going back downstairs to the lobby. He suspected the nurse's possible interference from his coming back up to speak with Lestrade. Holmes sat in the straight-back wooden chair between the bed and the window that looked out onto the hospital courtyard. Holmes checked the hour with his pocket watch while running through the cases in his head and formulated his questions for Lestrade.

An hour and twenty minutes later, Lestrade came through the door, assisted by an orderly who had him by the elbow. Lestrade's head was down as he gingerly took tentative steps through the doorway.

Sherlock Holmes made a coughing noise to let Lestrade know of his presence. The Inspector jerked his head, seeing Holmes seated at the bedside. "My God, Holmes. I'm so glad to see you here." Lestrade's voice sounded weak.

The orderly helped the Inspector back into bed and covered him with the blanket. "Stop fussing with me," Lestrade said to the man. "And tell the doctor I'm ready to get out of here." Lestrade felt embarrassed by his infirmity. The orderly smiled but left without comment. "Holmes, did you get the files from Grayson?"

Sherlock Holmes slid his chair closer to the bed, "Inspector Grayson gave me the nine files he had and told me he was unable to find the last three cases you were working on."

Lestrade bolted upright, then grabbed his head in pain. "I've had it with him," he swore. "You need to see everything." Lestrade looked as if he wanted to say too many thoughts simultaneously. His breath quickened, and finally, he dropped back into the raised pillows. "Inspector Grayson was supposed to report back to me the moment he gave you the files. I have yet to see him. Now I know why. The doctors threatened to tie me down to my bed yesterday because they found me dressed and escaping through the back door."

Holmes interrupted, "Where are the last three files?"

"The desk sergeant has them. That's what I told Grayson, too." Inspector Lestrade rubbed his face with both hands. "When I'm finished with him, he'll be chasing dogs with a net." Lestrade exhaled a deep, exasperated breath. "Holmes, we only have nine days left before this lunatic strikes again. I've got to get out of here."

Lestrade threw back the covers and swung his legs off the bed, but the dizziness from the concussion made him stop before getting up. He moaned and clutched his head again, trying to keep the room from spinning out of control.

Sherlock Holmes interceded and helped him back into a prone position, "I will keep you informed. For now, stay and recover. It wouldn't do to have you stumbling about. I'll go to Scotland Yard from here and get the files. Rest assured, I am closing in on the culprit."

Lestrade's face showed surprise. "You know who the killer is?"

"No, but I think I might know who the next victim is. Your case files will confirm my suspicions."

"When you go to the Yard, find Grayson and send him here regardless of the hour. I want to discuss his future as an Inspector."

Sherlock Holmes left Inspector Lestrade to fume from his bed. He would pass on the message but thought no more of the issue. Holmes stood curbside and hailed an empty carriage that was trotting by. "Take me to Scotland Yard and wait there until I return."

The carriage flowed with the early evening traffic. Small shops were closing for the night as the light faded with each passing block.

When the cab arrived, the driver had to let his fare off while stopped in the middle of the street. There was no place in sight to pull over.

The driver said to Holmes as he exited, "I'll keep going around the block until either a spot opens or I see you coming back out."

"I shouldn't be too long, ten minutes at most," Holmes said as he crossed the lane.

Several Bobbies had civilians in hand, one of the less desirable effects of the holidays. Sherlock Holmes could barely make his presence known with the clambering and shouting of store owners wanting justice and thieves pleading their innocence. He elbowed his way to the front counter and spoke loudly, "The desk sergeant has some files he is holding for Inspector Lestrade."

"I know who you are, Mr. Holmes. I've seen you here many times over the years. That dunderhead Grayson was supposed to pass these along to you. I'm sorry I wasn't on duty the other night. I should have known a simple task like this was still too challenging for Grayson." The Sargent leaned closer to Holmes, "Inspector Grayson is the nephew to the commissioner. I'm surprised he can find his way here in the morning. Don't tell anybody I said that. They'd have me walking a beat on the east side," he chuckled. The sergeant leaned down and reached for the papers under his station. "Good luck, Mr. Holmes. I read the files, and this guy is nuts."

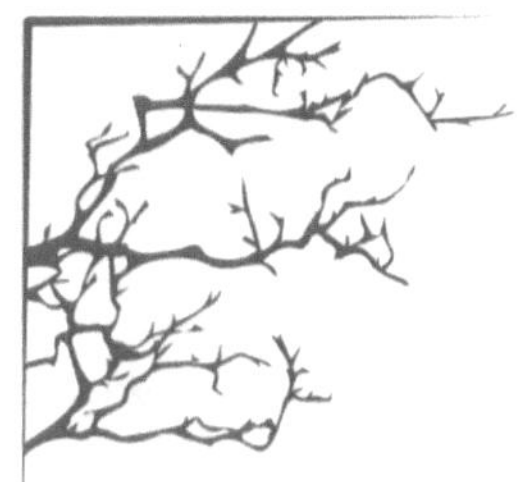

Chapter Eighteen

Dr. Watson sat at the kitchen table as he heard the familiar footfalls of Sherlock Holmes coming up the steps. Holmes entered and hung his coat on the rack, "What's that delicious smell," Holmes asked as he came through to the kitchen, suddenly realizing he was hungry.

"Mrs. Hudson appears to be on one of her cooking frenzies. She brought this up about twenty minutes ago. I was starving, so I went ahead and began without you since I had no idea where you had gone or how long you'd be away. Hope you don't mind," Watson said as he stuffed another forkful of stew into his mouth.

"Give me a minute, and I'll join you," Holmes spoke as he returned to the sitting room to drop off the folders. Moments later, Holmes came back and filled his plate. "Watson, I need your eyes tomorrow. Can you do that for me?" Holmes's voice conveyed a sense of urgency.

"Sounds important. You must know you can always count on me. What's our plan?"

Holmes explained, "Since our return, I have been working on what I believe to be, is a serial murder case."

"Whereas the two locations, we visited yesterday part of this investigation?" Watson asked.

"Yes, and I've been to three more since then. The killer made the first four murders appear to look like accidents—the sweep falling off the roof and tangling in his rope. The gardener tripped and fell into the fountain. Then, today, I investigated a site at Winterbourne Park. It was made to look like the victim had simply fallen over a root and hit his head. But it was physically impossible for that to happen that way. And he made the fourth murder to seem that the victim had got himself caught up in the machinery." Holmes took a few more bites from his plate and continued. "I'm telling you this so you'll understand the progression of the killer's boldness."

"I'm listening, Holmes," Watson said.

"The subsequent murder, though, was only slightly veiled to look like an accident, regardless of how Inspector Grayson labeled the case.

"And that was?" Watson asked again.

"A clockmaker's shop was in disarray, and the owner was asphyxiated with a pocket watch stuffed into his mouth."

"My God, Holmes. How cruel." Watson involuntarily put his hand to his mouth.

"Earlier this afternoon, I was reading the next case but have yet to investigate. The death is by strangulation using a G-string from the victim's violin. At this point, I realized a distinct pattern in the crimes."

"Yes," Watson said too loudly. "I saw the map you put up on the wall with the straight pins. I'm not quite there yet with the pattern, but tell me how I can help."

"I went to see Lestrade at Guy's hospital because only he knew where the other three files were. I'll read the remaining six files to confirm my hypothesis when we're finished with dinner. Your task, my friend, is to stake out the location where I believe the next victim will be." Watson nodded his acceptance. "To get a clear understanding of the criminal's motive and method, I'll need to investigate the other cases while you keep watching."

"Tell me where and when, and I'll do my best, Holmes."

"The where is St. Paul's Cathedral. I had the driver swing by the church on my way home, and I inquired about the priests residing there. I think the next victim is living there."

"Alright, who am I looking for?" Watson questioned.

"At the moment, I haven't enough evidence to make that determination. I want you to monitor those who appear to be casing the church grounds. I'm confident in your training by now that you can distinguish a suspicious person from the general populace."

Watson got up from the table and began removing the soiled dishes. "I wish I had more to go on than just suspicious activity, Holmes."

"Perhaps after reading the other reports, I'll have a better picture of the murderer to give you."

Sherlock Holmes poured himself a brandy and set the nightly fire in the sitting room while Watson volunteered to wash the dishes.

Once seated, he began reading the remaining files. Simon Graves, age forty-one, was found bludgeoned to death in an alley behind the apartment where he lived on the second floor. Graves had apparently been taking out his garbage in the predawn hours before leaving for work.

Inspector Grayson examined the clothing and found both his wallet and pocket watch undisturbed. Grayson assumed this was another robbery gone wrong, speculating the robber was frightened away by someone coming into the alley before he could make off with the goods.

Holmes scanned down the coroner's report and read that the victim's head received a catastrophic blow to the temple and died before his body hit the ground. However, the perpetrator continued to strike the body sixteen more times. He then used his hands to smear the victim's blood on the nearest brick wall, an entry door, and the casing. It appears the killer attempted to write words, but the surface was too rough to be precise. The Inspector could not decipher the message and made no note of what he could read.

Inspector Grayson noted an area twelve feet from the crime site had diluted blood mixed with water on the ground and a bloody towel tossed against the wall—a direct contradiction to Grayson's earlier conclusion.

Holmes looked up at the pinned map, seeing the pattern develop. He carried each new crime out with elevated brutality. The killer was no longer constrained by hiding his intent. And the crimes themselves were becoming more extreme.

The August first murder took place at Jeffery's Terrace. The victim's wife discovered her husband, John Bower, age sixty-eight, on her return from shopping that day. She told Inspector Grayson that she had left at approximately ten that morning and returned near dinner at around six pm. She was surprised not to find dinner on the table because her husband said he would bake salmon in the garden brick oven and have it ready by the time she returned. Grayson noted the tears she shed at the telling. *Holmes thought to himself, was this his explanation of her innocence?*

She searched throughout the house and finally went out to the gardens, hoping to find him, perhaps catching a nap. She discovered that someone tied his body to an oak tree at the far end of their estate. What she saw sent her into shock. The cause of death was four arrows penetrating Bower's chest. Above the victim's head, scrawled on the tree trunk, in the victim's blood: *"Considering what just happened, it pierced my heart and left me feeling weary with fear."*

Sherlock Holmes closed his eyes and rubbed them with his index fingers while tilting his head back towards the ceiling. A long sigh escaped under his breath.

"Are you alright, Holmes," Watson asked as he stood by his bedroom door. "You look as if you have the cares of the world on your shoulders."

"I'm fine, Watson." He paused. I could use a freshening of my drink since you're up." Holmes drank the last half ounce in his glass and handed it to Watson.

Other than the apparent connection by the names, Holmes was hard-pressed to identify the killer or even how to catch him. He held the September file in his hands, almost dreading opening it.

Watson observed him as he approached, saying, "Maybe you should take a break." He handed the brandy to his friend and sat in the chair next to Holmes.

"If I finish these tonight, I can do my investigation in the morning."

"Holmes, I understand the rush. The first of the month is ten days from now. But you need your rest to be effective."

"If I'm right, we have only two days to locate the killer. Look at the map," Holmes pointed his long, bony finger at it. "What do you see?"

"Oh, my God. Holmes, is that a... Cross?" Watson said with a gasp.

"Yes. And look at where the lines would intersect."

Watson knew this wasn't going to be good.

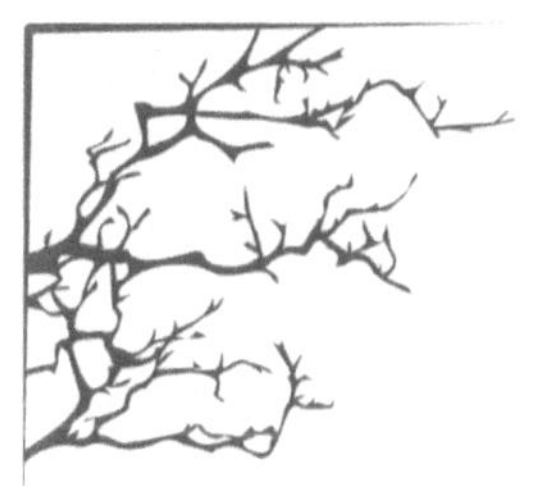

Chapter Nineteen

Watson got out of his chair and stood in front of the map. He drew his finger from left to right, then top to bottom. "It's St. Paul's Cathedral. That's why you want me there. You're hoping I just might get lucky and spot the killer." It finally dawned on Watson what Holmes had said earlier, but it had not sunk in that this was about to happen.

Watson stoked the fire and sat again by Holmes. "If you don't mind, I'll stay here quietly while you read the files." Their two-year friendship bonded these two men together, which words failed to describe.

"Thank you, Watson." That was all that he needed to say.

Holmes opened the September file and read, James Drew, age Forty-four, found in his home at Noble Street. Mr. Drew was a junior Vice-President at a local bank on Fleet Street.

When he failed to show up for work, they sent a teller to find out why. He told Inspector Grayson that he knocked on the front door for several minutes without an answer. The teller, Mr. Josh Green, thought to go around to the back of the house, hoping to see if the housekeeper was there. Mr. Green came to the back door and saw that someone had pried it open with some tool. He said he ran back to Noble Street and called for a Constable.

Constable Jenkins waited until he had a backup before entering the premises. They followed a trail of bloody footprints from the back door to their source. James Drew was lying in the middle of his sitting room, slit from his navel to his sternum.

Inspector Grayson came on the scene just before noon. His examination of the body suspected Mr. Drew was killed with a kitchen knife, though no evidence could be found in the house on any of the blades that matched the incision.

Other than finding the back door jimmied, Inspector Grayson could not assess a motive. The home had valuables throughout, including well-known artwork. Inspector Grayson interviewed the staff at Mr. Drew's bank, hoping to find the explanation there. In his report, Grayson assumed that bad blood between the bank and an irate customer caused this murder, and the case remains open.

Sherlock Holmes laid the file on the floor. He stretched his arms over his head and stood up. "I'm going to take a walk. Would you care to join me?" Holmes asked as he stepped over to the coat rack.

"Splendid idea, Holmes. I could do with stretching my legs."

The sun had set long ago, and the winter night air had a crisp bite. Holmes and Watson traveled north and walked into Regency Park. They saw only a few intrepid souls on the pathways because it was cold. Watson observed the pained expression on Holmes' face, and he asked, "What troubles you, Holmes?"

They walked for another minute before Holmes responded. "When I am a consulting detective for the cases I usually take, I find it is what I might call stimulating—locating a stolen jewel or finding a missing person. These diversions help fill what is sometimes a seemingly sedate lifestyle. Even on occasion, I have had to solve a violent crime, including murder." Holmes grew quiet for a moment before saying with a tinge of anger, "I can't understand why Lestrade sat on these cases for so long. He had to know Inspector Grayson was not up to the task. His taking over the case confirms the fact." Holmes wasn't expressing the turmoil and toll he felt reading these cases in sequence. In truth, they were feeling like a millstone around his neck.

Holmes and Watson walked for several more minutes before Holmes continued, "Lestrade has had three more murders that he thinks fit the Modus operandi. He should have contacted me months ago. I might have been able to solve the case before the tenth victim."

Watson looked at Holmes's shadowed face as they walked under the street lamp. "Holmes, there's something else. I can feel it."

Holmes pondered the question, "The mind of a serial killer. How did it come to be? Was he destined to his fate, or did it develop over years of...?" Holmes couldn't finish the thought. "It's troubling, Watson. I've read through nine of these police files, and I'm vexed. It troubles me to investigate twelve murders and knowing a thirteenth is at hand."

Sherlock Holmes and Dr. Watson completed their loop and returned to Baker Street. When they entered the apartment, Holmes said, "Thank you for your company, Watson. If you don't mind, I will read the last three files alone."

"Alright, Holmes. Then I'll say good night." Watson left the sitting room as Holmes braced himself for what would come from reading these last files. He prepared his pipe and sat in his wing-back chair.

The October first murder was at the residence of Thomas Cary, on Surry Row. Mr. Cary, age thirty, was known to be socially active. Cary used his wealth and handsome features to his advantage, according to his valet. Scandalous was the word the valet used. Inspector Lestrade asked what he meant. The valet told Lestrade that Mr. Cary often entertained young women at the residence and would give them access to his home, even when he was out of town.

Holmes skimmed through the report until he got to the crime scene. The victim died in his bedroom, tied to his canopy bedposts. Lestrade gave detailed information about the room and the position of the body. Cary had a piece of cloth wadded in his mouth to keep him from calling out.

The cause of death was multiple stab wounds to the chest, and the fatal blow most likely was to the heart. The killer used the victim's blood to write a message on the wall above the headboard, appearing to have used a quill to write with, and made a note of the fine penmanship.

"Deep into that darkness peering, long I stood there, wondering, fearing, doubting, dreaming dreams no mortal ever dared dream before."

Inspector Lestrade wrote the message in the report as part of the record. He felt the killer was now brazenly taunting Scotland Yard.

Sherlock Holmes put aside the file and took up November's folder. His nurse found Peter Weller, age eighty-one, at his residence in the posh district of Soho Square. The nurse, Miss Edwards, was quite overwrought by the discovery and had fainted at the sight of the carnage. After she recovered, she ran out of the house, pleading for help. A local Constable was flagged and took control of the crime scene.

Within an hour, Inspector Lestrade was at the site. Miss Edwards told Lestrade that Mr. Weller was a bit of a recluse and preferred little company. This seemed odd to Lestrade since Peter Weller had spent fifteen years in Parliament. He questioned the nurse about the daily routine and why Mr. Weller was left alone at night, considering his age.

She was quoted as saying, " Quite simply, he was a man of power and was used to getting his way. Who was I to argue?"

Sherlock Holmes turned to the last page to read the cause of death. Mr. Weller's carotid artery had been cut, and the victim bled out.

Inspector Lestrade made a note of the second message, written with the victim's blood on the wall, written in a five-line rhyme.

Sherlock Holmes picked up the last file, dated December 1st. The deceased Matthew Elliott was the same person Holmes had read about on the first day crossing the Atlantic on the Servia steamship.

Matthew Elliott was a retired chief of surgery from St. Bartholomew's Hospital and head of the medical school. But he was forced into retirement at the age of eighty-two. The newspaper report was highly accurate in its description of what took place.

Inspector Lestrade did include the taunting message written in blood, a five-line rhyme Sherlock Holmes did not need to read further. He had all the information he required to make his postulation.

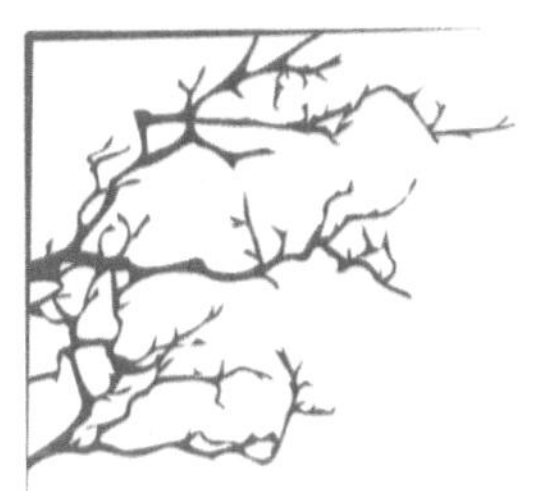

Chapter Twenty

Dr. Watson awoke to a melodic melody coming from Sherlock Holmes' violin. He wasn't sure but thought it was Mozart's First Concerto. He opened his bedroom door a crack and saw the lights had been extinguished and the embers in the fireplace casting a soft orange glow throughout the sitting room. Holmes sat on the edge of his chair, facing the fireplace, head bent into his instrument. A shadow aped Holmes on the back wall as his body swayed with the music. Watson thought of the famous quote from William Congreve – *music hath charms to soothe the savage breast. To soften rocks or bend the knotted oak.* It would not do to disturb Holmes. So Watson closed his door and returned to bed.

THE PUNGENT AROMA OF coffee drew Watson from his bedroom like a bee to a spring flower. He wrapped himself in his robe and followed the scent trail to the kitchen.

Holmes was dressed and at the table, already reading the morning paper. "Good morning, Holmes. I was hoping Mrs. Hudson would have prepared a hardy breakfast since I'll be out on the street all day."

"There'll be no need for that, Watson. There is a charming café across the street from the church's front steps. I'll be joining you."

"I thought you were going to investigate the other crime scenes and leave me on the lookout. But that said, I'm delighted to have the company. I was feeling rather uncomfortable with the task of picking out a needle in a haystack. You're much better at this than I am, Holmes," Watson said with relief.

"Watson, you underestimate yourself. You have a keen eye and a capable judge of character." Holmes picked up his newspaper and said, "Drink your coffee, and we can be on our way. Oh, and Watson, please bring your revolver."

SHERLOCK HOLMES AND Dr. Watson entered the quaint café just before nine a.m. They sat at a table that gave them an unrestricted view of the broad stone steps. Though the church service had already started, a few stragglers were still rushing in.

As Watson took his first bite of bacon, he asked, "Can you tell me, Holmes, about this murderous villain?"

First, Holmes picked up his table knife and was about to begin, as he buttered his scone, "Let's start from the beginning and build the profile. As you know, we saw the first victim was hung from the roof. After we circled the building, the sweep's ladder location would have been clearly on the backside of the building. I noticed the marking of years of chipping and scuffing on the placement against the tiles. The killer ascended the ladder unseen by the sweep and any potential witnesses sheltered by the roof's sloping angle from that location."

"The police report stated the sweep's chimney brush was found lodged in the flue. That tells me the victim was hard at work and grabbed from behind. The killer used a rope looped around the sweeps neck in a single motion and dragged him over the edge. Thus, the impression of an accident." Holmes ate his scone before continuing.

"The death at Fountain Cottage is interesting. First, Inspector Grayson missed the most obvious clue. There were two sets of prints in the hard, frozen snow, and he dismissed them as prints made during the investigation, even though the housekeeper had mentioned them when he first found the body. Then, the Inspector failed to get a formal statement from the housekeeper. He had asked about suspicious activity on the day of the murder, but we now know a couple appeared quite often up to that day, but not since, and this is the first indication that the victims were being cased."

"You mean it was premeditated?" Watson asked.

"Yes. The killer watched for his opportunity, and when it started to snow heavily, he seized the moment when the gardener approached near the fountain, and the view was obscured." Holmes took a bite of his eggs and wiped the corners of his mouth. He sipped his tea before going on.

"He killed the third victim at Winterbourne Park. He struck him in the head and moved the body to make it look like an accident. When I viewed the crime scene, there was no physical way for the deceased to have snagged his foot as he was positioned and hit the knot on the tree. Mr. Becket was five-ten, and he would have to be at least six-two to be killed in that fashion. I suspect the perpetrator hid behind the tree near the pathway and struck the victim with a blunt instrument. Then he dragged the body over to the tree with the knot, banged Mr. Becket's head to put blood on the tree, and then positioned the body with the leg firmly tangled into the knot."

Holmes gazed out the window as a man stopped for a few seconds in front of the church steps. A moment later, his wife and two children caught up with him. Watson smiled, "I'd assume that's not him."

Sherlock Holmes laughed. "No, but it would make an impressive cover. Shall I continue?"

"By all means, Holmes."

"The Four Mills murder is next, but I'll be brief. Mr. Chadsworth was last seen alive twenty minutes before the end of his shift while on the station, oiling the machinery. After interviewing witnesses, Chatsworth was evidently properly attired while oiling. Still, he was found wearing his coat and finding his cap at the foot of the machine when his body was discovered the next day. It would not do to speculate what led up to the crime, rather its conclusion. The killer took him from the dressing area and consummated his act by pushing Chatsworth into the cogs."

"Truly awful, Holmes," Watson said as he held his cup out for a refill.

"The next in line, Mr. Broadwick, was the first victim the killer made no pretense of staging an accident, despite Grayson's false conclusions. It also gave evidence that the killer used a woman to get close to his victim. We have already gone over all these cases, giving you an idea of our killer's mindset. With the restriction of time, I'm not going to investigate further. Other than, say, in Goldman's murder, there is no doubt in my mind the killer is using a woman for his purposes. According to the house cleaner's statement, Mr. Goldman was accustomed to having students come to his home. The last student was a young woman who most likely gained access to his house by receiving a key. The housekeeper said she was quite beautiful."

"Holmes, do you think she is taking part in these murders or is simply a pawn?"

Holmes was quick to answer, "Serial Killers tend to be loners and social misfits. I'd find it hard to believe he's doing this with her knowledge. The killer is getting a perverse pleasure in what he does, and it would minimize his gratification in sharing it with another person."

Watson interrupted, "Do you know who the next victim is? I understand the location by the cross-section of the map, but there are many opportunities on such a busy street."

"Elementary, my good Watson, the killer, created a cross with his chosen victims, as you saw. The next one will be a priest from this church."

Watson only now understood it wasn't just a cross-section, "And you know who?" Watson asked.

At that moment, the parishioners began to file through the door as the service ended. Seconds later, an elderly priest walked outside to shake hands with those leaving. "Look up at the entry. That is the next intended victim." Something caught Holmes's eye. "Time to go, Watson." Sherlock Holmes stood and dropped money on the table, and Watson barely had time to retrieve his hat and coat and still keep pace with Holmes.

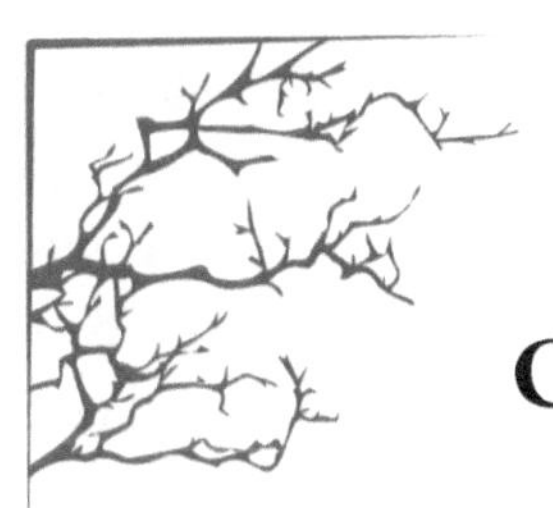

Chapter Twenty-One

"Where are we going, Holmes?" Watson called out as he flew through the café door.

Sherlock Holmes turned right and set a quick pace towards Ludgate Hill, staying close to the edge of the buildings. When he reached the corner, he stopped, his head swinging back and forth. The mid-day street traffic was daunting, with horses and wagons competing for space on the busy streets.

Watson caught up with Holmes, "What's the matter, Holmes," he asked breathlessly.

"I'm sure I saw our man," he said and proceeded to step out into the heavy traffic, weaving his way between the wagons crossing Ludgate Hill.

Watson took his life in hand and dashed several steps behind his friend. The beating of iron shoes and the squelch of wagon wheels filled the air. Sherlock Holmes jumped back as a dray cart charged forward at the midpoint of the lane. The driver pulled hard on the horse's reins and stood in a single motion, trying to impede his progress so as not to run over a pedestrian. "Coulda killed you, mate. Ain't your mother teach you anythin'?" he yelled at Holmes.

Holmes' attention was singularly focused on his suspect as he ran around the front of the horses as Watson said to the driver, "Sorry." And he, too, scooted around the twin pair of beasts as they stomped their hoofs in agitation.

Holmes saw his target turn left down a narrow street. The man was a block away as he stood at the curb. Not wanting to alert the prey, Holmes walked faster than pedestrians' flow, but not enough to be noticed. He turned on Creed Lane and slowed his pace.

"Which one is he, Holmes?" Watson was now striding alongside, looking for an obvious target.

"Halfway down the block, Gray woolen tweed jacket. Coal-black pants and black Victorian top hat."

"Yes, yes, I see him," Watson affirmed.

Holmes and Watson maintained their distance while following their suspect, who at this moment made a quick left turn again onto Carter Lane. They quickened their steps until they came to the corner. Sherlock Holmes peeked in the direction of the man's movement. A hundred feet ahead of them, their suspect walked with leisure, but his eyes surveyed his surroundings, looking for anything that might be out of place.

"When we go around the corner, we'll window shop. Just follow my lead," Holmes said as he stepped out from the building's corner.

They strolled like Sunday shoppers, hesitating in front of the massive plate-glass windows displayed with wares that not even Holmes had any idea of their use. After two long blocks, the suspect opened a storefront door and entered, making a quick glance towards Holmes and Watson and forming a grin on his face.

Holmes began to run with Watson at his heel. They covered the distance in less than twenty seconds and passed through the same door. Inside the spacious three-story main floor, crowds of shoppers flowed in all directions. Holmes turned in a circle, looking for the man. Because Sherlock Holmes was taller than average at over six feet, he could see reasonably over the crowd.

A brief moment of anxiousness in him swelled as Holmes scanned the room. "There," he said over the din to Watson. "He's exiting through another door. This building apparently spanned a third of the block and fronted Godliman Street.

Holmes and Watson moved into the current in that direction and moments later felt the cold, fresh air on their faces as they came out the door.

The suspect had sped up and was almost to St. Paul's Church Yard. Sherlock Holmes matched his speed, calling over his shoulder, "Watson, he must have caught on to us. Hurry."

As they reached St. Paul's Church Yard, Sherlock Holmes spotted the man jumping aboard an omnibus. They were too far away to catch up with it, but several more were going in the same direction.

Holmes flagged a bus, and they climbed aboard. "Watson, keep a lookout on that side; he could get off at any point along the way."

Watson had caught his breath and asked, "Holmes, how do you know this is our man?"

"I had been watching him pacing the street in front of St. Paul's for the last half-hour. When the service was over, he took a particular interest in the priest when he came out with the parishioners." Watson still had a puzzled look. "His evasive street maneuvers seem to confirm my assessment." This, Watson could understand.

"Do we have the evidence to make a citizen's arrest?"

Holmes laughed, "Watson, you are developing into a detective, after all." Watson grinned like a Cheshire cat. "In answer to your question, no. But I intend to follow him to wherever he is residing and make a plan to catch him red-handed."

The buses travel through the city, with people getting on and off at each stop. Holmes strained at the neck as their bus fell further behind. They were less than a mile from the river when the suspect leaped off the omnibus, ran past the corner building, and disappeared around the corner. "He's on the move," Holmes said as he jumped off the moving bus, his feet in motion as they hit the ground.

Watson was blocked by a one-legged man with his crutch lying across the aisle, which caused Watson to trip when he attempted to get by. By the time he had regained his feet and departed the bus, Sherlock Holmes was in sight. Dr. Watson walked up the street, looking at each intersecting avenue that merged, hoping to see Holmes in pursuit.

After ten blocks up and back, Watson gave up. He couldn't think of what to do next, but he saw a corner pub with full-size windows facing the avenue and decided to wait for Sherlock Holmes to reappear while having a pint of bitters to quench his thirst.

One pint turned into two, and lunch followed an hour later. It looked like Watson was on his own. When he finished his meal, he hailed a hansom to take him back to Baker Street. There, he would wait for Holmes' return.

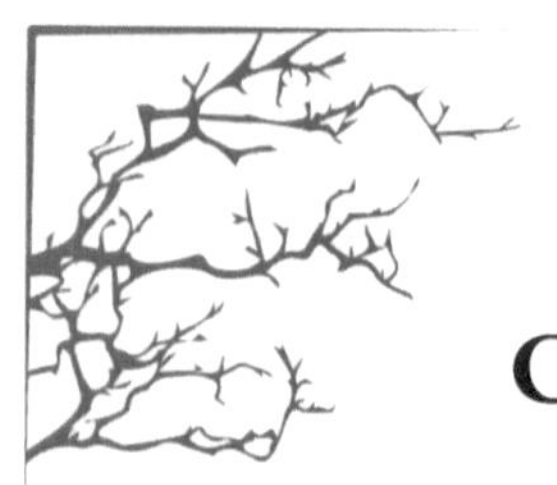

Chapter Twenty-Two

Several hours after nightfall, Watson was sitting in his comfortable chair by the fire. Holmes had been gone for too long, and Watson started to worry. He had asked Mrs. Hudson to prepare a dinner for Holmes, but it was now sitting on the kitchen table, cold. It wasn't as if this was the first time Holmes disappeared and slipped in during the wee hours of the morning, but Watson knew his friend was chasing after a serial killer, and Holmes was unarmed. For a moment, he found himself angry with Holmes. Why was it he was the bearer of arms? How many times had Holmes said to him to be sure to bring his revolver? And why couldn't Holmes carry his pistol? Watson knew Holmes was proficient at boxing and an accomplished swordsman, but these are modern times, and no one wears a rapier at their side anymore.

Watson suddenly burst out laughing at the image of Sherlock Holmes wearing a three-corner hat with a peacock feather, a long cape, and a diamond-studded sword. He felt like he was mothering Holmes as he said to the flames, "Holmes is quite capable of taking care of himself."

He got up, poured himself a brandy, and took a book from the shelf. Holmes would be fine, he kept telling himself. Watson then stoked the fire and settled in for the evening. Within minutes, Watson's chin rested on his chest as he softly snored.

Footsteps alerted Watson to Sherlock Holmes' return; they were a welcome relief. Holmes hung his coat and joined Watson in the sitting room. He sat heavily in his chair, looking tired.

"From the way you look, I take it you were unsuccessful in your pursuit?" Watson said.

Holmes smiled, "If one could admire a killer, I would give him his due credit." Watson's brows rose in surprise. "He's no fool. When he caught on to our shadowing him, he was as elusive as any man I have ever chased. After a while, I felt as if he were playing a game of cat and mouse. There were times when I thought I'd lost him only to find he had hesitated at some corner or passed through a door, allowing me to see his escape." Holmes interrupted his narrative while he filled his pipe. "The pursuit edged ever closer towards the river, then he disappeared into thin air. It had been like pursuing an apparition." Sherlock Holmes lit his pipe and stared into the fire.

"What do you intend to do now, Holmes?"

Holmes slipped off his shoes and put his feet up on the ottoman, saying, "Finish my pipe, eat a cold dinner, and sleep on it."

THOUGH WATSON ROSE early, Holmes was already in the kitchen making tea. "I've got your coffee ready to brew," Holmes said.

"Mighty decent of you, Holmes." Watson began to brew. Have you got a plan yet?"

"I'm torn, Watson. If I notify Scotland Yard that I believe the serial killer will strike at St. Paul's, they'll be swarming like ants at a picnic, and we'll miss catching the killer. On the other hand, I think Inspector Grayson is too inept to handle the task, and therefore, in all likelihood, the priest will die, and I'll still miss catching the killer. Unfortunately, they have not released Lestrade from the hospital. At least he has some competency."

"Tell me what I can do to help, Holmes."

"Well, if you don't mind, go downstairs and get the morning paper." Holmes put the boiling water into the teapot and poured a small amount of milk into his cup. Watson smiled at the thought that Holmes sometimes took things so literally.

Watson came back with the Times and a tray, "Sometimes, I think Mrs. Hudson is as intuitive as you are. As I reentered the door, she met me at the landing and handed me this," Watson set the tray on the kitchen table.

Holmes looked at it with a furrowed brow, "What is it?"

"She called it Buche de Noel and wished us a Merry Christmas. Then she said she would be gone on Christmas morning and wouldn't be able to give it to us then."

Watson took out two plates and cut slices from the yule log as Holmes opened the newspaper. Sherlock Holmes was silent and had touched neither his tea nor his culinary gift.

A minute passed before he lowered the paper. "He's dead. The priest died late last night," Holmes stated.

Watson looked stunned, "What? How did he do it, and when?"

"No, you misunderstand me, Watson. The priest wasn't murdered. It says here, Father Christo, a priest at St. Paul's Cathedral, died of an apparent heart attack while supping with the other priests." Holmes stood up, "I need to go to St. Paul's. I only hope they haven't cleaned the priest's utensils yet." Holmes was out the door before Watson could respond.

SHERLOCK HOLMES RETURNED several hours later carrying a large parcel. "Hello, Watson. I was just in time; the parsonage was still in disarray. They had yet to clear the dining table from last night's dinner. When I explained why I was there, they were very reluctant to believe me, but I finally prevailed." Holmes opened the bag and spread out the dishes and cups that had been in front of the dead priest. "If you'll excuse me, I'll be doing some chemical testing on these. Though I doubt the killer would use poison to kill the priest, it's best to eliminate the possibility."

Watson thought it best to vacate the apartment, knowing the process would take most of the day. And the chemicals often emitted a pungent odor.

"Holmes, on my way out, I'll stop by Mrs. Hudson's door and ask her to fix you dinner later. I know how you get when you have your nose stuck in a test tube." Holmes didn't reply, and Watson wasn't even sure he had heard him since he was already focused on the job.

Chapter Twenty-Three

Dr. Watson entered the apartment and saw Holmes sitting in his chair, staring into the fireplace, lost in another world. He removed his scarf, coat, and hat, hanging them on the wrought-iron rack stand. He looked in the kitchen and saw the sparse remains of Pigeon in white sauce and the crust from a venison pie still sitting on the kitchen table. "At least you ate. I'm surprised." Watson was still rubbing his hands when he asked, "Can I fix you some tea, Holmes?"

Sherlock Holmes continued looking at the flames, saying, "The tests were negative, no sign of any form of poison."

Watson asked, "Can I pour you a glass of port? It complements what you had for supper."

Holmes gave a single nod while Watson poured. Watson edged over to his chair with the two glasses in hand and handed Holmes the dark red liquid. "Thank you, Watson."

They sat quietly for several minutes as the fire glowed, giving off a comforting warmth. "So, where does this leave us, Holmes?" Watson asked.

"I can only imagine the rage that must be going through the killer's mind. He directed this series of brutal murders for this moment and this specific victim and took an entire year, methodically killing twelve men on the first of each month. Now it has unraveled before his eyes."

"Does that mean he will simply disappear, or will he concoct another spree?"

"No doubt he'll continue to kill, but this is an obsession. His focus is single-minded on completing the cycle." Holmes thought for a moment, "He will have to find a legitimate replacement for the priest, someone to be the surrogate."

"Do you mean another priest?" said I.

"That remains a possibility but not likely. And not within the next two days of Christmas Eve and Christmas Day. Part of the drive to kill is taking pleasure in the planning. He took a month for each, and a day wouldn't do."

Watson finished his drink, saying, "This is beyond me, Holmes. I can't get into the mind of a psychopath. And how you do it, it's a wonder you don't drive yourself crazy."

"It does take a toll, Watson. It does take a toll." Holmes set down his drink and ritualistically filled and lit his pipe. By doing so, Watson smiled to himself, watching Holmes do the very thing that kept Sherlock Holmes sane.

AN EARLY MORNING KNOCK on the entry door roused Watson from a warm bed. He could hear Sherlock Holmes greet someone and thank them. Watson dressed, and before leaving his bedroom, he picked up a wrapped package, tucking it under his arm.

Watson came around the corner to the kitchen where Holmes was unloading a tray prepared with a holiday breakfast. "Mrs. Hudson has outdone herself this morning, a meal to rival café Royal on Regent Street. She had this prepared for us as she was about to leave."

"It's lovely, Holmes. Perhaps we should use the good china this morning. It isn't often we have cause."

As Watson suggested, they set an elegant table to match the fare. Once seated, Watson put the wrapped package on the table near Holmes' right elbow, "A Merry Christmas, Holmes."

Holmes smiled at Watson. "Wait one moment, Watson. I didn't forget," said he as Holmes jumped up from his seat and quickly left the room. Watson could hear a drawer opening and closing before Holmes' return.

Sherlock Holmes set a teak box and a small, wrapped package by Watson. "Go ahead, Watson," he pointed to the gifts.

First, Watson opened the box and found two dozen cigars finely wrapped in gold foil. "They're Cuban," said Holmes. Next, Watson unwrapped the package and saw a silver flask with the inscription – Dr. John H. Watson—inscribed across the face.

"Holmes, I'm touched," said I. "Now you open yours."

Holmes undid the ribbon and carefully unwrapped the package. Then he unfolded the white tissue paper and picked up a plaid patterned deerstalker hat. "Thank You, Watson. I'll treasure it."

Watson smiled, saying, "I found it at Macy's in New York. It just spoke to me. I'm delighted you like it, Holmes." Then Watson turned serious, "Well, Holmes, what do we do now?" Watson assumed they would begin a new search for the serial killer.

"We get dressed and go to church."

Watson's eyebrows rose, "What? I'm surprised. I never thought of you as a particularly religious man, Holmes."

Sherlock Holmes gave Watson a wry smile. "We are going to go to St. Paul's Cathedral."

"Yes, I'm sure they have a lovely Christmas service. Give me a few minutes to wash up and dress properly, and then I'll be ready." As he picked up the dishes and set them on the counter, Watson said. "I'll take care of these when we get back."

DR. JOHN WATSON HAD not attended a church service since before his deployment to Afghanistan. He wore his dress uniform on that occasion, as did every officer and enlisted man. But today, he opened his wardrobe closet and looked inside for inspiration. Watson chose medium gray woolen trousers, a dark gray waistcoat, a white linen shirt, a knee-length oxford brown frock, and a black silk ascot. His boots were highly polished, and he would grab his black silk-trimmed top hat before going out the door.

Watson came out of his bedroom to find Holmes already putting on his brown plaid cloak and wearing the same suit he had put on this morning. "Aren't you a dandy," Holmes said to Watson. Laughing, he added, "Perhaps we should find a wedding to attend after the church service."

Sherlock Holmes put on his Christmas gift that turned out to match his cloak, though Watson was unaware of it at the time of his purchase. Watson stood by his bedroom door, now worried he would be overdressed. Holmes chuckled, "Are you coming or not, Watson?"

Watson smiled and adjusted his ascot as he followed Holmes out the entry door.

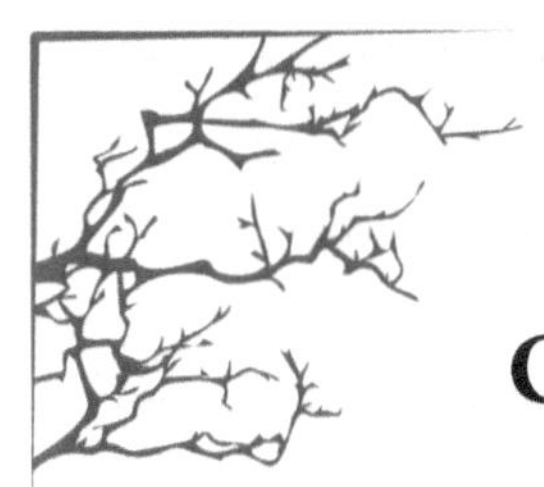

Chapter Twenty-Four

The carriage arrived at the front steps of St. Paul's Cathedral and deposited Holmes and Watson. The time was ten-thirty-five, and they were twenty-five minutes early for the eleven o'clock service.

Watson was puzzled as to why they had come so early. It seemed out of character for Sherlock Holmes to go somewhere and have to sit and wait for the upcoming event.

They entered through the center entry door with twenty-three minutes to wait. Holmes walked down the center aisle, bypassing rows of empty seats. Watson is surprised as they continue towards the front. Watson expected the seats would soon fill within the next ten minutes, and Holmes seemed to have a specific idea of where he wanted to sit.

As they came to the front pew near the altar, Holmes chose the second row on the left, four seats in. Watson sat next to him and watched as the remaining benches quickly filled. Holmes sat quietly, hands folded in his lap, and his eyes were ever-moving as he scanned the sanctuary.

Watson looked up at the Cathedral dome's dizzying height, a hundred- and eleven meters overhead. It gave Watson a feeling of vertigo, and he had to look away. His eyes focused on the wrought iron candle stands lining both sides of the sanctuary. Each held a dozen lit candles, giving a soft glow to the immense space.

The pipe organ played Silent Night in a slow, methodical movement from above on the second level. The parishioner's voices quieted, and a procession of young boys clothed in white robes solemnly walked down the center aisle carrying lit candles and silver crosses. Watson was awestruck.

Watson leaned in close to his friend and whispered, "This is spectacular, Holmes."

At that moment, Sherlock Holmes had his eyes fixed, looking up at a candlelit halo hanging over the altar. It hung from the arch thirty feet overhead on long woven cords. He appeared not to have heard Watson's comment.

The priest invoked the congregation to stand when Holmes said, "Follow me." He stood and slid by those sitting to the right. A few heads turned as they watched them head to the stairwell.

Watson followed Holmes as he climbed the stairs, trying not to make noise on the stone's steps, though to Watson, they sounded like rushing water over rocks. They came out onto the balcony opposite the organ. Holmes moved slowly towards the balcony wall, his eyes looking out and not at the people below. He stopped a few feet short, then visually followed something that Watson couldn't see from where he was standing. His head tilted up as Holmes closed the distance to the wall. He then looked straight down and saw the priest directly below, prostrating over the altar.

Just as quietly, Holmes took several steps backward and moved towards the inner wall, feeling it with his right hand, concentration edged on his face. His hand gently fingered the texture until they stopped at a point six and a half feet above the floor and three feet to the left of the balcony.

Watson came alongside Holmes to see what he had found. "What is it, Holmes?" whispered I. Watson could see a one-and-a-half-inch diameter metal ring that was snugly fitted against the wall.

"A trigger, Watson. Best not touch it."

Sherlock Holmes walked around the room's perimeter and found a narrow door that blended into the room's architecture. "Watson, I want you to stay here. I don't expect anyone to come up, but if you find yourself with a lone man, I want you to draw attention to others even if you have to interrupt the service." Holmes located the recessed handle and opened the door.

"I don't understand what is happening," Watson said, alarmed.

"Be patient, and I'll explain everything when I get back." With that, Holmes disappeared through the door, shutting it behind him.

A chamber no more than three feet wide circled the dome's interior. Holmes lit a match and followed the narrow hall. Twenty paces in, he found another door, a bit wider and stouter. He turned the knob as it opened outward.

Sherlock Holmes stood outside on the cathedral's rooftop. A narrow maintenance walkway ran along the ridge line but without handrails. In the cold, moist weather, Holmes moved cautiously, a step at a time. His arms outstretched for balance, he kept his eyes on each foot placement.

He was halfway across when he took a step that hit a patch of ice. Holmes suddenly lost balance and fell forward, arms flailing in the air. He hit the ridge hard and slid to the left as a third of his body now hung over the steep slope. Holmes grabbed the copper cap with both hands and held it tight. Pulling himself onto the ledge center, he could once again stand.

Holmes finished the trek to the bell tower and searched for an opening. The door was on the north side of the building, and when he pulled the handle, it opened effortlessly. He examined the lock and saw that the killer had pinned it with a nail to keep it from locking.

Sherlock Holmes stood in the bell tower for a minute, viewing the city from this grand height. He breathed in the chilly air and thanked the heavens for his narrow escape from certain death. But there was work to be done. So, he descended the stairs to the main floor, surprising a young priest who attended the bells at the proper time.

"May I help You," the priest asked.

"No, thank you. I was momentarily disoriented," Holmes said, hoping to escape without further questions.

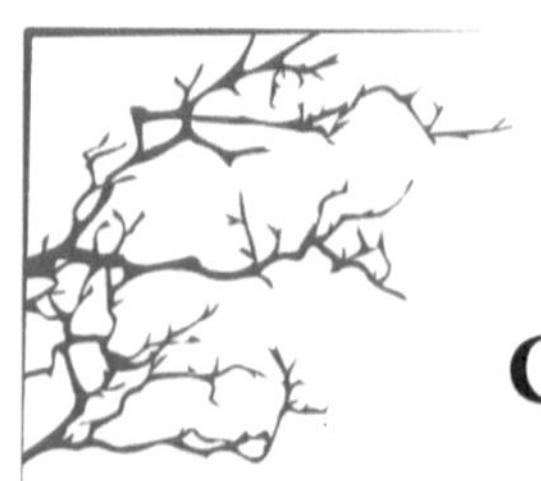

Chapter Twenty-Five

Dr. Watson had moved to the balcony rail to watch the ongoing service, but with his body turned to keep an eye on the stairwell. It had been at least fifteen minutes since Holmes's departure, and Watson began to worry.

It was the cape and deerstalker hat that drew Watson's attention as Holmes worked his way through the standing congregation along the outer aisle and headed for the stairway. His footsteps were a welcome relief. When he reached the top of the stairs, Watson said, whispering, "I did not know where you disappeared to."

"I'm sorry, Watson. I'll explain everything after the church service." Holmes stood beside Dr. Watson at the balcony rail like two cherub angels overseeing the Christmas Eve service.

AN INTONATION CAME from the priest, and the congregation stood for the last song. After which, the people receded like an outgoing tide. "Watson, it is time we met the priest," Holmes said as he made for the stairs.

It took quite a while before the priest could leave his post at the front door. There were many hands to shake with the merriest of Christmas wishes. Holmes and Watson stood against the vestibule wall, patiently waiting to speak with him.

With a sigh of a job well done, the priest saw the two men waiting. "Good morning, I'm Father Calkins," the priest extended his hand.

Holmes took a hand in his and said, "This is my associate, Dr. Watson, and my name is Sherlock Holmes."

Father Calkins' eye grew bright, "Mr. Sherlock Holmes, I have read of your adventures for years. And Your Watson, the scribe of these intriguing tales. I can't tell you how excited I am to meet you both." The expression on the priest changed, "I couldn't help but see the two of you up on the balcony during our Christmas service. Are you, by any chance, on a case?" The Father grinned with anticipation. "Perhaps you are in search of a jewel thief or a counterfeiter?"

Holmes said, "Father Calkins, if I may, please come with me into the sanctuary, and I'll explain."

They walked down the center aisle to the altar. Holmes stopped and turned to them. "Father, can you have someone bring a wood crate here for a demonstration?"

Father Calkins waved over a youthful altar boy cleaning debris left by the parishioners. "Would you and Robert go to Father Riche's office and bring the empty wood box in the corner?"

The two boys left for a few minutes before returning with a thirty-inch squared box. "I need you to place it on the altar here," Holmes pointed to the exact location.

"Oh, let me remove the altar cloth before you do that, my boys," Father Calkins said as he quickly came forward.

After they set it, the Father asked, "Tell me, Mr. Holmes, what you intend with the box?"

Sherlock Holmes grinned. "I'd prefer to show you. Please stand back here," Holmes indicated, an area away from the altar. Then he headed to the stairs, all eyes watching him.

Holmes came to the balcony and said, "Stay exactly where you are." He reached his left hand straight out behind the wall, looping his index and middle fingers into the ring, and pulled.

A long, slender silver cross was at the center of the hanging halo. When Holmes pulled the cord, the cross detached and plummeted straight down the thirty feet and pierced through the wood box to its hilt.

Those standing below involuntarily jumped back when they saw the silver streak flash downward and crash with a resounding crunch into the wood.

Father Calkins gasped, "Oh my Lord in Heaven," his hands clasping his face and his breath labored.

It took less than a minute for Holmes to come back downstairs and witness the stunned expressions on all those around the altar.

"What... What is the meaning of this?" the priest stammered.

"Perhaps you should sit down," Holmes said to the priest, whose body shook like a leaf. He led him over to the front pew and steadied him as the body slumped into the contours of the bench.

"I am going to ask you a few questions, if I may." Father Calkins slowly nodded his head. "It is essential for me to know when the church was decorated for the holiday season and specifically the hanging of the halo."

The priest's eyes glazed over, trying to concentrate. "It was an anonymous gift that I assumed was from a member of our congregation. I never personally met with him. All I know is that he came about a month ago and did the installation himself." Father Calkins's brows creased, "Mr. Holmes, how did you know?"

"Dr. Watson and I have been investigating a series of murders that have occurred over the last year. The culmination of the killer's sinister plan was to be a very public display. Each victim was chosen and executed in sequence by name and location, all pointing to his finale here at St. Paul's. He had planned to kill your senior pastor, Father Christo, either on Christmas Eve or Christmas Day."

First, the priest's eyes grew wide and then teared up. Holmes continued, "With the unexpected passing of Father Christo, it has foiled his plans for the time being. However, I expect he'll find a way to complete his task." Holmes handed the priest his handkerchief.

"Dr. Watson and I came this morning to make sure he would not proceed despite the change in priests. It was only a matter of time before we found his method for completion. I had Dr. Watson posted at the trigger point while I investigated his planned escape route."

It was more than the priest could take in. "I still don't understand his motive." Tears trickled down the wrinkled face.

Too bluntly, Holmes said, "His motivation was for Father Christo to be a substitute for Christ's crucifixion on the cross. When the priest genuflects over the altar, the sword-shaped cross was meant to pinion him to the altar."

A long gasp escaped from the priest. "Oh, God. What possesses a man to do something so evil and cruel?"

Sherlock Holmes could only look at the grief-stricken priest but had no answers.

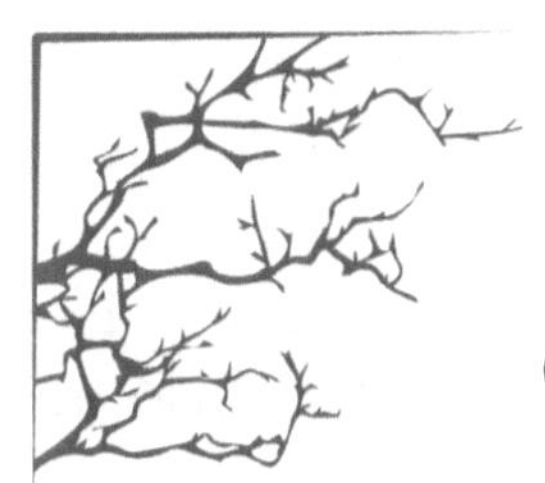

Chapter Twenty-Six

Dr. Watson and Sherlock Holmes returned to their apartment on Baker Street, finding a platter from Mrs. Hudson at their doorstep. Watson unlocked the door as Holmes carried in the tray. She had prepared a traditional English dinner for them, and it was still warm.

Watson took the note pinned on the tray. It read, "Mrs. Hudson asked us to deliver this at noon. She said you often had a meal prepared for you at this hour. Merry Christmas."

"I hope we gave Mrs. Hudson an appropriate Christmas gift this year. She has undoubtedly been generous with her cooking lately," Holmes said as he took down plates from the cupboard.

"Interesting that you should say that, Holmes. We did indeed give her a wonderful gift. Two days ago, a cast-iron cook stove got delivered to her door," Watson said with a sly grin.

Holmes burst out laughing, "That explains the sudden increase of hot dishes at our doorstep."

Watson joined in the laughter, "I hadn't at the time considered the ramifications, nor that we would benefit in such a magnanimous manner."

After their dinner, Watson yawned and stretched his arms out. "This reminds me of my days eating in the officer's mess. We never knew when our next meal would come, so we stuffed ourselves and shuttled back to our barracks to sleep off the effects, as I'm about to do now." Watson stood, helped clear the table, and retreated to his bedroom.

Sherlock Holmes bundled up before leaving the apartment. What started as a walk to clear his mind soon turned into him trying to figure out how to find the serial killer. With their presence at the Cathedral and the disarming of the weapon, the killer would need to act quickly to find an appropriate victim.

Holmes had two agendas; first, to ascertain who would replace Father Christo and locate the killer before he could kill again.

Holmes hailed a hansom cab and gave the driver instructions to take him to where he had last seen the killer. He thought if he could walk those streets, he might gain some insight into where the killer was hiding.

The driver dropped Holmes off on the corner of Commercial Road East and Waney Street. "Thank you; I'll walk from here." Holmes paid the driver and headed south on Waney.

Intuitively, Sherlock Holmes wound through the streets and alleys in a southerly direction. After a couple of hours, he neared the river and its abundance of warehouses. Holmes knew this would be an area where few questions would be asked by those working within their confines.

Holmes was cold from being out on the streets for hours with a harsh wind coming off the river. He finally stopped in a small pub on Mercer Street to take off the chill. A warm fire blazed in one corner, crowded with patrons, and a handful of men stood near the dartboards in a friendly game with beers in hand. He sat at a table that a drunken longshoreman recently vacated. Peanut shells littered the floor at Holmes' feet.

A barmaid dressed somewhat provocatively with more cleavage than was proper in Victorian society came to take his order. "Please bring me a sherry," Holmes said.

"What the hell is a sherry? We have ale, rum, or whiskey. If you want something else, you can go back uptown," she spat out, looking at Holmes' upscale attire.

Holmes smiled at her, saying, "An ale well would be excellent." He rubbed his hands to get back the circulation and took in the hardened faces of people who had labored all their lives with calloused hands.

The barmaid returned with a tall mug and a foamy head that spilled over on the table. "Two-pence," she said as if Holmes would not pay.

He did. While Holmes nursed his ale, he ran through each case in his mind, looking for clues that had not been evident before. From the first moment he saw the list of names, he saw the beginning pattern. Then, as he read each case, he found the location pattern. That led to St. Paul's Cathedral.

But where does the killer turn to now? This Holmes did not know and had nothing to glean from the other deaths. Then there was the question: did the killer have an unwitting accomplice? And there was a lack of any consistent description by witnesses.

Logic dictated only one conclusion. The killer was proficient at disguising. Holmes drank past the foam and set it back on the table. He checked off the list, Fountain Cottage, a couple who appeared older. A workman was walking freely at the mill, and a disabled person visited the clock shop. The other murders had no witnesses, but the killer could have used a disguise to come close to the victim in all likelihood.

Holmes had warmed up considerably. He finished his drink and was ready to leave. Upon exiting, Holmes turned right and continued towards the river in his zig-zag pattern, crossing High Street several times, now heading east. If asked, he couldn't say what exactly he was looking for and certainly wasn't expecting to run into the killer. But he felt a connection to this general area.

Sherlock Holmes ended up by the river at Bell Wharf. He stood at the river's edge, looking out, watching the commerce. Leaning against a stout keg, Holmes took out his pipe and had a smoke. He thought to himself, was his pursuit a red herring the other day? Had the killer led him away from his lair like a bird protecting her chicks? Without further evidence to work with, he was walking in ever-wider circles.

Holmes finished his smoke, knocked out the ash on the edge of the keg, and traveled back to High Street to catch a cab home.

Chapter Twenty-Seven

Four blocks from where Sherlock Holmes had been smoking his pipe, a lone man sat in the dark, brooding. His mind raced with conflicting thoughts. For an entire year, his plans worked like clockwork. There wasn't a day he hadn't delighted in his accomplishment. The sheer artistry of his creation would go down in the annals of history. Not even Mary Ann Cotton could hold a candle to him for what he had done and was yet to do.

Years earlier, Mary Ann Cotton had killed twenty-one people, including most of her children. And for what? Money. She'd marry, then poison her husband for the insurance. But she got caught.

Still in the dark, a smile formed on his face. He knew Mary Ann before she married her second husband. He lived next door and knew early on that she was giving her children arsenic. From his bedroom window on the second floor, he would watch as Mary Ann would put a small portion of the poison onto a child's food until they succumbed to the sickness.

He realized it was because Mary Ann Cotton was both a pleasant-looking woman and she presented herself as genteel that she avoided the usual suspicions. Society dictated that someone who murders for pleasure should look the part. That was the first lesson he took to heart.

He did not need money; all the wealth he required was at his disposal, and that gave him an advantage. His accommodations were paid for outright, with no one to knock on his door. He could do as he pleased. He had chosen his location a year before he had begun his project. He arranged all the necessary improvements and had private access no one could identify.

The killer was like a cancer cell in the center of a body. Millions of residents, but his location was isolated and apart from the bloodstream of the city. He could freely move about undetected and infect at his pleasure.

Enough brooding. He lit several candles and admired the handiwork displayed on a city map. It was beautiful, symmetric, and even poetic in its execution. Then, the anger crowded in. Fate had played a wicked role in smearing ink onto his Rembrandt. On whom could he take revenge?

A crystal decanter held a Cabernet Sauvignon. He poured a glass and examined the ruby-red color—a color he loved even from childhood. He had to admit it was an obsession, but he forbade himself from having anything in his possession linked to it. It had to be a private, personal, and secret pleasure. He thought back to his youth and the first time he drew blood.

When his father took him on his first hunting trip, he was between eight and nine years old. The hours of trudging through brush bored him to distraction, but his father ignored the boy's complaints. Then, somewhere around eleven thirty that morning, his father sank low into the bushes, and they waited quietly. On the rise, a small herd of deer crested the horizon. His father aimed a four-point and, with one shot, brought it down cleanly.

When he stood over the fallen deer, his father handed him a sharp six-inch blade and instructed him in the appropriate way of dressing game. At that moment, when his hands felt the warm, sticky blood, his heartbeat faster, and his breathing quickened. The pure joy of it coursed through his veins. Nothing could make his father prouder than having his son partake in such a manly way, but he never knew the obsession triggered that day.

When and how would he draw blood again? The month was nearing the end, and he hadn't found his next victim yet. Yes, the city was full of hapless souls, and he had limitless opportunities to kill. But where was the symmetry of that?

He had to set these thoughts aside and get dressed for dinner. Tonight, he would be taking Hillary to The Criterion Theatre, an underground restaurant in Piccadilly Circus.

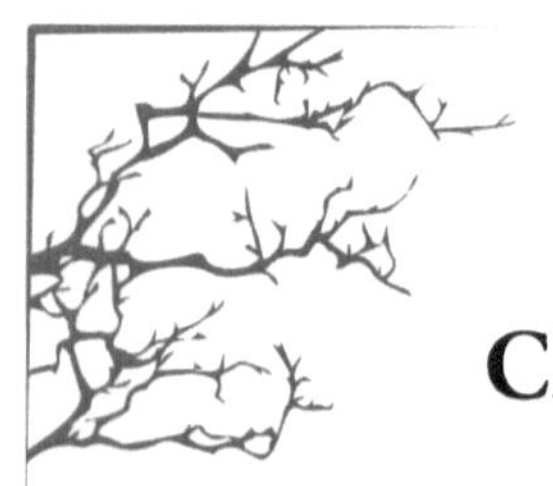

Chapter Twenty-Eight

Sherlock Holmes sat quietly in his sitting room chair, rereading each file, looking to glean additional information. But when he reached the end, he knew he had missed nothing. His conclusions remained the same, and it was incumbent upon him to identify the next victim. The parameters were too narrow to find a replacement. The same was true for the killer.

Watson bound up the stairs and entered, carrying a box. "Well, hello, Holmes. When did you get back?" he asked while setting the box on the floor by his chair.

"A while ago. Long enough to reread these reports."

"Holmes, I have lived with you for some time now. I know very well how you get when you're on a case, but this is different. You said it yourself that it takes a toll. And there is nothing more you can do tonight." Watson took out a new pair of shoes from the box and put them on. "I think we should go out for a late supper."

"Alright, Watson," Holmes said, laying the files on the side table. "Give me a few minutes to dress."

WATSON HAILED THE HANSOM while Holmes dropped off Mrs. Hudson's tray at their door. When Holmes climbed aboard, Watson told the driver the address on Piccadilly Circus.

"Piccadilly Circus? I thought we were having supper on the Strand," Holmes said, surprised.

Watson laughed, "Trust me, Holmes, it's a splendid restaurant." Watson looked thoughtful for a moment, then said, "You know, it was there that I had met with a friend for drinks. And while we were reminiscing, a young man named Stamford, a dresser from Barts, tapped me on the shoulder. It was he who recommended my contacting you in the first place when I was seeking shared lodging."

"Best decision you ever made," Holmes said, looking smug.

"Holmes, you made a joke. See, I knew going out to supper would do you good." Watson took pleasure in the one-upmanship.

The cab stopped in front of the arched entrance, and the number of people coming and going indicated that they would need to wait for supper.

"Holmes, order me a brandy at the bar while I run upstairs to make our reservations," Watson said as they came through the door.

Holmes studied the over-lavished tilework throughout the main floor. It was not his taste in décor, but the general public seemed to like it, judging by the crowded rooms.

Watson Found Holmes standing at the far end of the bar with his head in a cloud of smoke as he puffed away with a lit match on the cigar's end. Holmes said, "I assume our seating will be a while, so I got these to go with the drinks." Holmes handed Watson his glass and a cigar.

"Mighty decent of you, Holmes," Watson said as he removed the foil and bit off the end, then lighting it with a flourish.

OUTSIDE THE MAIN ENTRANCE, a man wearing soiled and tattered clothing edged within fifteen feet of the Criterion's door, hoping for a handout. Patrons passed him as if he were invisible. He had about given up hope when a carriage pulled up, and a well-dressed couple opened the door to exit. She was wearing a purple full-length satin dress with a long black cape, and he was in a black tux and top hat.

As they stepped out of the carriage, an employee of the restaurant came out to shoo away the beggar. "You've got to move on, mate," the man said.

The beggar began to shuffle away when the tuxedoed man drew a half-crown out of his pocket and gave it to the beggar.

"Thank you, sir. Tonight, I won't freeze in the alley," he said.

The woman slipped her arm into the crooked elbow of the tuxedoed man, saying, "How kind of you, Sir Lancelot."

"We all must do what we can," said the killer.

The couple entered the door and stood at the cloakroom counter, leaving behind their coats.

SHERLOCK HOLMES EXHALED a cloud of smoke facing towards the front of the bar. He witnessed the couple as they came in and studied the man's face. A full salt and pepper beard obscured most of his features, but something about the shape of the nose and spacing of the eyes gave Holmes pause.

The couple walked away and took the stairs down to the theater, arm in arm.

"Watson, come with me," Holmes said as he put his drink on the counter and placed his cigar on top of his glass.

Watson stood motionless for a moment, trying to decide if he should leave his cigar and drink or bring them along. Holmes was already about to go around the corner when Watson set his brandy down and laid his cigar into the ashtray, still smoldering.

Holmes and Dr. Watson pushed through the crowded room and descended the stairs towards the theater. It took several minutes to get to the main level, and they saw the seats were quickly being filled. Watson followed Holmes, first down the left-side aisle, then up the center aisle while looking along the rows of seats.

"Did you see the suspect?" Watson asked breathlessly, figuring this was the cause.

"I'm almost positive. He's wearing a black tux and is accompanying a woman in purple satin."

When Holmes got to the back row, he stood on the tip of his toes, looking over the bobbing heads. Still, he didn't see them. Holmes hurried down the right-side aisle to the base of the stage and scanned from there. He was now sure the suspect was not on the main floor. "Watson, we will look at the first balcony next. Keep a sharp eye," Holmes said as he dashed back up the right aisle.

"MY DEAR, SOMETHING doesn't agree with me. Do you mind if we leave?" the killer questioned while watching the men who had chased him scanning the theater audience.

"I'm sorry, of course, we can go," she said, gathering her dress to climb the four steps in the second-floor balcony's box seats.

The couple swiftly made for the stairs and collected their coats. The killer frantically waved a carriage to the curb and helped Hillary into the coach. The killer's heartbeat was hard and fast, but not from fear. It was the hunt, whether hunter or prey; it didn't matter.

SHERLOCK HOLMES AND Dr. Watson thoroughly searched the first and second balconies, but they came up empty. "Do we search again, Holmes?"

"No," said he. "It was impossible to have kept a low profile while quickly walking up and down the aisles. Wherever they were seated, they obviously saw our moves and escaped."

"What now," said I.

"We have supper."

They returned to the bar and found their drinks and smoldering cigars where they had left them.

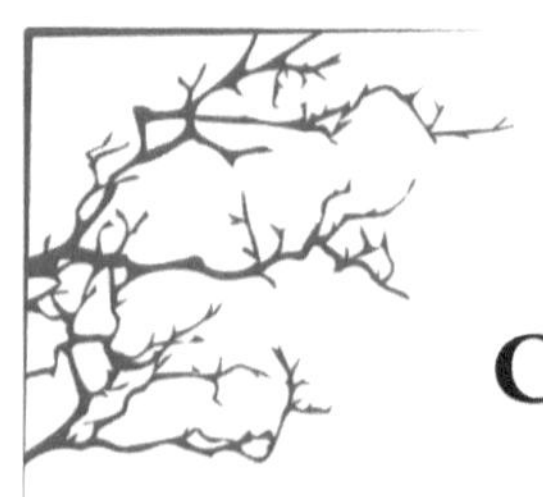

Chapter Twenty-Nine

Christmas morning, but neither Watson nor Holmes was in a merry mood. Twice, they lost the suspect in a crowd. Considering they were clueless about who the next victim would be, what are the chances they would have another opportunity to apprehend the killer?

Watson was up and had the coffee brewing. Holmes' tea kettle was beginning to whistle when Holmes came into the kitchen.

"Mrs. Hudson's neighbor has delivered another tray this morning," Watson said. "There is a note on it thanking us again for the generous gift, and she had made us a Christmas quiche."

Holmes smiled, "If she keeps this up, we'll have to start buying her groceries to make up the cost of her cooking for us." He poured the boiling water into the teapot and sat at the table. "If the killer stays true to form, we only have seven days left to either find him or identify the victim."

Watson put a plate of food in front of his friend, saying, "We can deal with that later. Eat now."

Both men ate in silence, keeping to their thoughts. When they finished, Holmes went to the front steps, hoping they had delivered the newspaper despite a light snow cover during the night. He found the rolled paper leaning against the outer door casing and sheltered from the flakes that continued to fall.

Holmes poured another cup of tea and took it into the sitting room to read by the fire. He was about a half-hour into the newspaper when Watson heard Holmes shout, "Eureka."

Watson came out of his bedroom, still in his dressing gown, not having dressed for the day. "What is it, Holmes?" He asked.

"Watson, get dressed. We are paying Inspector Lestrade a visit." Holmes jumped out of his chair and rushed to his bedroom.

SAFELY IN HIS SHELTER that felt like a secure cocoon, the killer had just returned from breakfast with an early morning edition of the newspaper. He had been all smiles at the well-wishers as they said Merry Christmas. But in truth, he saw himself more like Ebeneezer Scrooge, wishing he could have them all boiled in their pudding. He hated that his mother insisted the family sit in the parlor while reading from that insipid book. One Christmas, when he was twelve, he took the book off the shelf and tossed it into the fire—then denied knowing what happened to it.

A dozen candles were lit, but one remained dark. He looked forward to the day that, too, would glow with satisfaction. A warm wool blanket lay across his lap as he opened the newspaper. He had almost finished it before he saw the article. A sinister grin grew on his face, and he said to himself, "Hail Mary and Joseph."

SHERLOCK HOLMES AND Dr. Watson arrived at Guy's hospital and made their way to Inspector Lestrade's second-floor room. The Inspector was sitting in a chair, reading reports delivered by Inspector Grayson. "Holmes, Watson, I'm glad to see you. Tell me you have good news."

Holmes said, "Lestrade, how much longer are you going to be here?"

"If you're willing to help me, as long as it takes to get dressed and assisted out the front door," Lestrade said, tossing the file on the unmade bed.

"Watson," Holmes began, "go find a carriage and meet us out front. We should be there in ten minutes or less." Watson nodded and quickly left.

Inspector Lestrade moved stiffly as he put on his clothes. "Help me with my jacket, won't you, Holmes?" Lestrade held out his right arm for Holmes to slide his arm through the sleeve. "If you take me by the elbow," the Inspector raised his right arm, "I'll be fine."

Sherlock Holmes handed the loose files for Lestrade to carry and took the proffered arm. "What about your belongings?" Holmes asked.

A telltale sneer appeared, "Grayson can come back and get them. I'm pretty sure he can't foul that up."

The Inspector and Holmes slipped through the hallway undetected and walked gingerly down the steps to the first floor. Holmes peeked through the door, looking for the nurse at the lobby desk. "Wait," Holmes held up his hand to Lestrade.

Holmes watched as the desk nurse spoke with someone and pointed them in a direction. The person shrugged their shoulders as if not understanding. The nurse let out a gush of air and said, "Just follow me." She rose and led the man out of the lobby.

"Now," Holmes said as he pushed open the door, and they hurried through the lobby before her return.

Watson stood with the carriage door open at the front entrance. He helped Inspector Lestrade into the cab and climbed in after him. When Holmes boarded, Watson said, "I didn't know where to tell the driver to go."

Sherlock Holmes turned to Lestrade, saying, "If you are up to it, Scotland Yard."

With bravado, the Inspector said, "I'm prepared to siege the Bastion if needed."

Scotland Yard was unusually quiet on this holiday. When the party arrived and entered the lobby, the desk sergeant stood from his stool and greeted the Inspector, "Sir, I'm surprised to see you. We didn't think they would release you for another week." The sergeant came around the counter to shake hands with Lestrade. "A Merry Christmas to you, sir."

"Christmas?" Lestrade said. "I forgot what day this is. Merry Christmas to you too, Sargent Addison."

The Inspector led the way to his office and nearly collapsed into his chair. "All right, Holmes, you have waited to tell me until we arrived. Do you have the killer ready to be presented wrapped up in a bow?"

Holmes just shook his head at the Inspector's humor. "First, Inspector, do you have access to government floor plans, specifically the National Gallery?" Holmes asked.

Lestrade smiled ruefully, "They're not in my file cabinet, but yes, I can get ahold of detailed floor plans. And the reason, you ask?"

"In this morning's newspaper, there is an announcement of a gala New Year's Eve event being held at the gallery. I believe that will be the new finale for the serial killer. He wants a spectacular conclusion to his spree."

Inspector Lestrade interrupted, "But how do you make this connection? He could continue with the home invasions indefinitely."

"It fits the pattern. His victims' deaths became bolder with each murder. The cover of possible accidents for the first four was like a drug-induced high. But, like heroin, it took more to produce the same effect. Thus, the crimes became clear; they were murdered. When that wasn't enough, he quoted Poe out of context to fit the thrill he felt with the bloodletting. With the last two murders, he began taunting Scotland Yard, feeling invincible."

"How do you do it, Holmes?" Inspector Lestrade asked. I had all the same information as you, but it appeared jumbled."

"Don't be too hard on yourself. You have many other cases to attend to simultaneously while I can focus my singular attention on the subject at hand. What you don't know is the failed attempt at St. Paul's Cathedral."

Lestrade put his face into his hands and asked between fingers, "I'm almost afraid to ask."

"The intended victim was a priest who was to officiate at the morning Christmas Eve service. But the priest died of natural causes the day before. Watson and I attended the service just in case he chose to follow through with his plan. Then, after the service, we removed the trap he had set."

"Oh my, God. Was he planning to kill the priest with a thousand witnesses?"

"Yes. Now you can see the logic in the culmination of a replacement victim at the National Gallery."

"What do you want us to do, Holmes?"

"When you have the floor plans, bring them to Baker Street, and we'll go from there."

"It will take some doing with offices closed, but I'll be at your residence within the hour," Inspector Lestrade said.

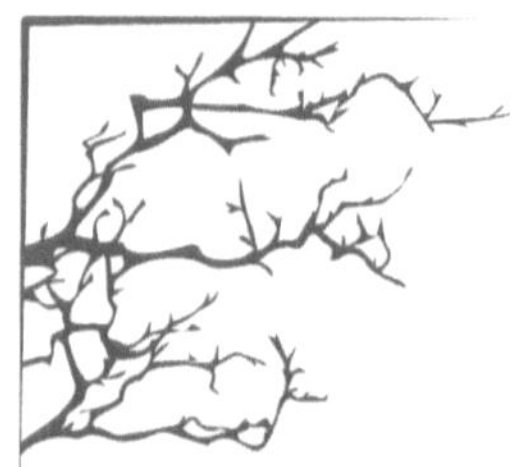

Chapter Thirty

D r. Watson had just poured the tea water into the pot when the Inspector stepped out of the hansom with an armload of rolled papers. "Watson," Holmes said. "We'll need a third cup. Inspector Lestrade is just now coming up the stairs."

Holmes met the Inspector at the door and led him into the sitting room, where he had a table cleared for the floor plans. Lestrade set out the plans, saying, "I have two sets here. One is for the second level, and the other is for the main floor."

Sherlock Holmes moved the second-floor plans on top and traced the rooms with his fingers. "According to the newspaper, this room here," he tapped it with his index finger, "is where the New Year's Eve gala will take place."

"Thank you, Holmes. We'll have officers at every door by tomorrow," the Inspector said.

Holmes smiled, "All in good time, Lestrade. But for now, I want you to keep everything exactly as it is: no more police and no less. I don't want to tip our hand. The killer knows someone was on his trail when Watson and I pursued him a couple of days ago, but I lost him near the river. I need to find him before he stages the next murder. We don't have enough forensic evidence to link him to this series of killings to date. If I can find where he is hiding, then perhaps we'll find what we need to convict him. As you know, serial killers tend to keep trophies of their kill." Holmes poured tea for Lestrade.

"How do you intend to find him, Holmes?"

"When the gallery opens tomorrow, I'll be there and wait for him to show. I must assume he has seen the same article and will go there to assess the layout and make his plans."

"Won't he recognize you when he comes in?" Lestrade asked.

"You have, on many occasions, seen me in disguise. I'm not concerned that he'll identify me. I will appear like one of many art appreciators wandering through the galleries. It is apparent the killer is also proficient at disguises. I almost missed seeing him at Criterion's last night. Unfortunately, he spotted us searching the theater and left before we could follow him."

Inspector Lestrade scratched behind his ear hard, "Do you know who the killer is, Holmes?"

"Yes, and no. I know of him. Now I have a face to put with it."

"It seems to me if we apprehend him now, it would be the safer. Then, try to piece together the evidence to convict. What if he succeeds in this murder and goes underground again until he concocts a whole new scenario for a killing spree?" Lestrade asked.

"It is for that very reason we must lay a trap for him. If I fail to locate where he is hiding within the next few days, we can reassess our plan. But for now, I ask you to trust me."

WHEN THE DOORS OPENED, the killer was already planning to be at the National Gallery. A laugh escaped into the open space as he said slowly, "And I know just how I'll do it."

Dressed for lunch, he slipped out of his shelter and walked a half mile before he hailed a carriage. He was to meet Hillary at Kettner's. Upon arrival, he found Hillary seated at a table in the corner, away from the windows. She knew that when they had not dressed up in disguise, he preferred out-of-the-way locations, and this was the best she could do.

"Hello, love," he said, taking a seat with his back to the room.

Hillary lifted a package off the floor and placed it in front of him. "Merry Christmas, love," she said with a warm smile.

He stared at her a moment as if she were not there, then caught himself and put on a smile. He reached into his inner jacket pocket and brought out a small, wrapped box.

Hillary's eyes glistened with delight. "Oh my, I can't imagine what it could be," she said as she began to unwrap the gift. Inside the box lay a red ruby pendant on a delicate gold chain. It's lovely." She wanted to lean across the table and kiss him, but he would not allow this. "Open yours; I think you'll like it."

He pulled on the ribbons but finally picked up a table knife to cut them. The knife slipped, cutting an inch-wide opening on his thumb. At first, the gash was a pale white trench of flesh but quickly filled, then overflowed with blood. He stared at it, mesmerized, not hearing Hillary screaming.

Holding his hand up near his face, he let the blood trickle down his arm and drip onto the white linen tablecloth, creating a crimson pool below his elbow. The waiter, seeing the accident, rushed over to wrap his hand in a towel. It took all the killer's willpower not to push the waiter aside and free his glorious hand.

He looked at Hillary's stricken face and smiled. "It's nothing. Shall we eat?" The blood-stained package remained unopened.

His good humor surprised Hillary, considering what happened. He appeared to be jollier than she had seen him in weeks.

It was the right time to ask a question: "Can you come up and stay with my family over the New Year's holiday? After all, you are my distant cousin, and they need not know of our relationship."

He thought to himself, relationship? Is that what you call this? "My dear, I would love nothing more than to sit in your parlor and celebrate the new year with your family, but I have an obligation that cannot be changed." Her look was crestfallen, and tears welled at the edge of her eyes. "But I tell you what. Tomorrow, before you catch the train home, let's have some fun dressing up. I have something in mind that you will love."

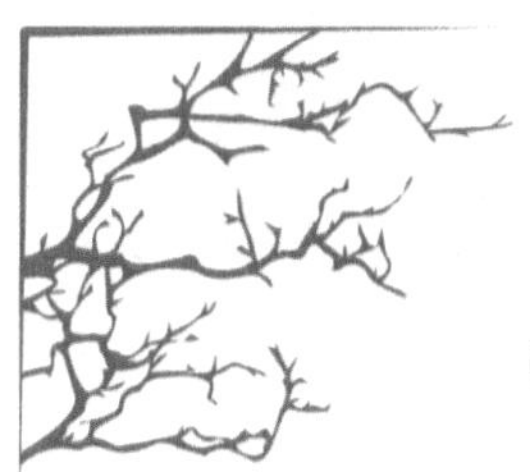

Chapter Thirty-One

D r. Watson sat at the kitchen table, having his first cup of coffee. His head rose as he heard sounds of drawers opening and closing from within Holmes' room. A prolonged silence occurred before he perceived Holmes's distinct footsteps coming through the sitting room towards the kitchen. To Watson's surprise, Holmes appeared to look like a very rotund gentleman with full cocoa-brown sideburns clear down to the jaw. His eyebrows match in color and thickness.

"Well, Watson, how do I look," said he with a smile.

"Holmes, if I hadn't seen you here in our home, I'd never recognized you." Watson stood up and squished on Holmes' beard. "Is this real hair," he asked.

Sherlock Holmes laughed, "Yes, I had it made some time ago and have been saving it for such an occasion as this."

"And the clothes?" Watson said.

"They came from that little shop around the corner that sells used clothing. I stopped in yesterday thinking I might have use for them."

"Ingenious, Holmes, simply ingenious. Give me a few minutes to get dressed, and I'll be ready to come with you."

"Not today, Watson. I should go alone. If I locate his hiding place, then I would welcome your presence alongside me."

A NONDESCRIPT DOGCART carrying Hillary turned off High Street onto Glamis Road and drove to a dilapidated area of warehouses near the river's edge. She paid the driver, who said to her, "Are you sure you want to be left here? It doesn't look safe to me. And personally, I certainly wouldn't walk alone in any parts here, even if you paid me."

She just smiled at him, saying, "I will be perfectly fine. Thank you."

After the driver disappeared around the corner, Hillary looked in both directions and walked down the street. She edged over to a side alley and vanished. Once inside the building, she followed the weak light to where he was waiting.

"Did you follow my directions?" he asked, his voice a bit sharp.

"Yes, I walked several blocks before taking a dog cart here. Then I waited until the driver left before coming in," she said, a bit defensively. Of course, he knew the second part because he had watched from the third-floor window.

His demeanor suddenly brightened, "Here is what we are going to do today," he said as he took her to one of many racks of clothing. "I think you'll find something that will fit nicely," he said, holding out a men's gray frock coat.

Hillary began to giggle, "You want me to dress like a man?" she said, holding the frock up against her chest and walking back and forth with a Manish stride.

He smiled, "Yes, I told you we were going to have some fun. Now hurry; we haven't much time, and I want to get there by the time the doors open."

"But where are we going?"

"You will see. Get dressed."

By the time Hillary finished, he had come out behind a screen wearing fashionable women's attire. His hands were covered with white gloves pulled up to his elbows and heeled lace-up boots. She clapped her hands to her face, gasping, "My, God. You're beautiful. I'm almost jealous. Let me have a look at you." He pirouetted in slow motion, pleased with the effect.

He looked closely at her and said, "You need one more accouterment," speaking the last word with a French accent. He took a narrow box from a drawer and lifted the lid. He then attached a curled handlebar mustache using a sticky liquid that smelled unpleasant. "Perfect," he said.

They left the warehouse and strolled leisurely northward to Cable Street. Hillary took his hand in hers and perfected her stride, taking long steps like a man.

It took him several blocks to get the hang of walking in heels. He almost tripped twice and was glad she had taken his hand.

Before they hailed a carriage, he said to her, "Remember, you are the gentleman and must speak for us."

Her eyes showed glee at playing this game. She threw back her shoulders and gruffly coughed to get into character. Then, wiggling her mustache, she waved her arms at an approaching coach. As the driver pulled up to them, she was about to give directions but hesitated, not knowing where they were going.

The killer leaned close to her ear and whispered, "National Gallery."

Hillary almost squealed but caught herself. She harrumphed again and spoke in as deep of a voice as she could muster, saying, "Take us to the National Gallery on Trafalgar Square, if you please."

She opened the coach door and let him in first. Then stepped in and banged the side of the coach, as she had seen some men do on occasion.

SHERLOCK HOLMES ARRIVED ten minutes before the doors opened to the gallery. He stood across the street at Trafalgar Square, watching for any telltale sign. When the hour struck, he saw a guard inside the front door turning the lock. Holmes hurried across the street and entered.

Within a few minutes, other patrons began filtering through the entry. Holmes took up a position in the corner near a large oil painting of sheep in a field surrounded by majestic snow-covered mountains. He pretended to study the oil while keeping one eye on the entrance.

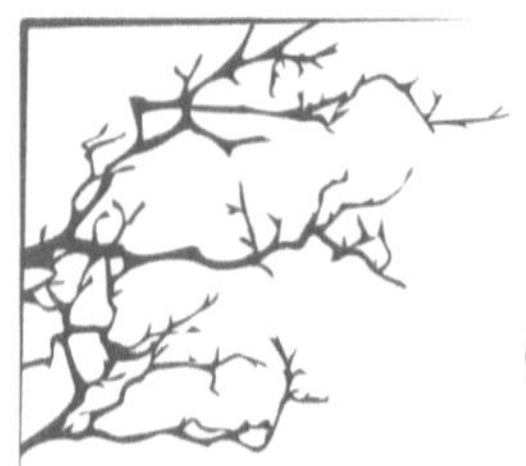

Chapter Thirty-Two

The carriage drew up in front of the gallery at a quarter past the hour, and the couple departed the coach. Hand-in-hand, they climbed the broad stairs and smiled at the guard protecting the entry.

The killer precisely knew where he wanted to go as he directed Hillary to the right, using the held hand. They moved slowly and stopped at several paintings before they neared the stairs to the second floor.

Sherlock Holmes had seen the couple enter and hadn't given them any more thought. But when they moved purposefully towards the stairs, he watched closely. It wasn't until he saw the woman's profile that he made the connection. The subtle shape of the nose and the angle of the chin gave Holmes pause. Holmes realized the magnificent disguise and even admired it.

Holmes waited several minutes to allow them to move away from the top of the stairs. He then ascended, taking the steps slowly. At the top of the stairs, he saw the couple casually moving towards the north vestibule. Eventually, that would lead to the Octagonal Hall, where the New Year gala was scheduled.

Sherlock Holmes added a waddle to his gait as if his thighs continually rubbed. He followed them at a distance into the north vestibule, keeping his eyes on the gallery paintings.

At the midpoint of the hallway, Holmes turned left into a smaller alcove that was still in the line of sight with the Octagonal Hall. There, he could observe the couple safely through the series of open gallery doors.

HILLARY WAS QUITE ENJOYING herself. She felt the inner pocket of her coat, hoping there would be a cigar tucked away. She knew they would never allow her to light it in the gallery, but it would have been fun to chew on it in a manly manner.

The killer played his part well. He had his right arm looped through Hillary's crooked left arm. He gazed at the paintings, but his real attention was on the structure of the room. He gauged the height of the dome and looked for access points. He wanted to target his chosen victim exclusively, but the interior had many limitations. And with the shortness of time, he saw only one alternative.

SHERLOCK HOLMES WATCHED the killer scanning the room and how he had paid particular attention to the dome. Holmes would have to come back and personally assess the likely attack scenario.

Holmes could tell the killer saw what he had come for and was tugging on his companion's arm. They turned towards the door and walked in Holmes' direction.

Sherlock Holmes turned his back to the door and moved in front of a classic oil portrait of a fifteenth-century Prussian king.

THE KILLER HAD SEEN enough. He whispered in Hillary's ear, "Don't want to be late for your train," he said, gentling, pulling on her arm.

Hillary began to frown but stopped short when she saw the kindled anger rising in his eyes. "Perhaps you're right, my dear. It's just that I was so enjoying our game."

The couple retraced their steps and descended the stairs they had come up twenty minutes earlier. Exiting, they walked across the street and passed through Trafalgar Square. Midway through the park, he stopped and looked back to see if they had been followed. Satisfied, he continued towards Strand Street. They walked east until they could hail a carriage.

SHERLOCK HOLMES STOOD just inside the gallery entrance door, watching the pair strolling through the square. When the killer stopped, he quickly backed away from view. He waited until the couple turned onto the Strand before leaving. The coach Holmes had come in was parked next to the Union Club west of the Square. He quickly made for the carriage and climbed in. He instructed the driver to follow the described couple at a safe distance.

The couple continued east until they stood in front of Adelphi Theatre, where they found a coach for hire.

Holmes' driver pulled to the curb a block past the theater and waited until the couple drove by. "What now, Mr. Holmes?" The driver asked.

"Stay far enough back just to keep them within sight, and if their carriage stops, do the same thing as before and go a block further. If need be, I'll get out and follow by foot, and you can keep a distance from me just in case I need you again."

"Yes, sir, Mr. Holmes."

Holmes followed them east and southward until their carriage stopped at the corner of Cable and Cannon Street. The couple disembarked and continued walking on Cable Street, then turned right onto Victoria.

Holmes knocked on the coach's ceiling, signaling the driver to stop. He jumped out and reminded the driver to keep his distance. By the time he came around the corner, the couple had vanished.

Sherlock Holmes felt perplexed. How was the killer achieving his disappearance? Holmes walked down one side of Victoria Street and back up on the other side. There was no sign of the couple and no obvious route of escape. All the side streets were dead-ended, but he looked through each to see if he had missed anything.

The coach waited for him on the corner while he did his search. When no satisfactory answer came, he returned and instructed the driver to the nearest telegraph office.

Sherlock Holmes sent a wire to Henry Marc Brunel, son of Isambard Brunel, the famous engineer, asking if he could direct Holmes to specific information. And that it was imperative to have a prompt response.

Mr. Brunel replied swiftly. By the time Holmes returned to Baker Street, a cablegram was waiting for him.

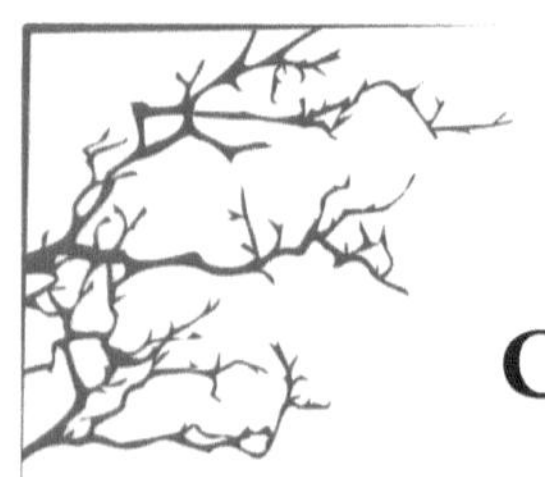

Chapter Thirty-Three

It was late afternoon before Holmes returned a second time to Baker Street. He had a set of large, thirty inches by thirty inches leather-bound books with him.

Through the window, Watson saw Holmes was carrying a heavy burden and opened the lower level door for him. "A bit of light reading, Holmes?" he asked with a smile.

Something distracted Holmes like a bloodhound on a hot-scented trail, and they didn't reply. He mounted the stairs two at a time and went directly into the kitchen, where he pushed aside the newspaper on the kitchen table and opened the first book.

Watson asked, "Is there anything I can do to help?"

"Would you mind asking Mrs. Hudson if she could make a plate of sandwiches? I think this could take some time."

Holmes had all three volumes spread out and opened as he referred back and forth, turning pages and making notes. It wasn't until late in the evening that Holmes finally closed the books and found Watson reading a magazine in the sitting room by the fire's glow.

"Watson," said he. "Tomorrow, I shall be gone in the morning but will come back probably by ten to pick you up if you're available."

"Of course, Holmes. I'll be dressed and ready for whatever is required of me." Watson responded.

IN THE EARLY MORNING hours, the killer began loading a drey cart with the tools and boxes he had acquired the previous day. Before the city was fully awake, he left his lair and traveled the streets with light traffic.

The National Gallery would not open for another three hours. He parked his wagon near the service entrance and left it while having breakfast at a small café on Pall Mall East.

THE SAME DRAPE-COVERED coach returned for Holmes the next day. They again parked across from the Gallery next to Trafalgar Square. There, Holmes waited for any sign of the suspect. They had opened the Gallery doors for less than twenty minutes when Sherlock Holmes spotted a silhouette on the rooftop.

Stepping out of the coach, Holmes said to the driver, "I will return in a few minutes. When I do, take me back to Baker Street, and we'll pick up Dr. Watson."

Holmes crossed over to the National Gallery and walked to the corner of the building. He leaned forward with only his head past the edge, looking to be sure the suspect had not come off the roof. Holmes moved swiftly, crossing the thirty feet to the horse tied to the post. Holmes stepped up to the drey cart, threw back the cover, and looked inside. The canvas-covered wagon had boxes, ropes, and ladders. He opened the first box and saw what he had suspected it might be. It would take the killer some time to rig his devices. So Holmes closed the box and left.

DR. WATSON SAT BESIDE the front window, smoking his third cigarette, anticipating his friend's imminent return. When he saw the carriage coming down the street, he put on his coat and hat while descending the stairs and met them curbside. He had barely climbed in before the horses galloped away.

"What's the rush, Holmes," Watson asked.

"We only have a few hours to find where the killer resides."

Watson almost laughed at the impossibility of it. "Holmes, there are four and a half million people who live in London. How are we to find one location on such notice?"

"My dear, Watson. I do wish you would pay attention. We followed the suspect going east before he knew he was being followed on our first encounter. Then, yesterday, I followed him and a young woman to an area that further narrowed the search. That led me to get the books you saw me studying. I have narrowed it down to a few square blocks with that information."

Their carriage arrived, coming east on High Street. Holmes signaled the driver to pull over when they reached Glamis Road. "Wait for us here," Holmes ordered. Then, they scanned their surroundings. "This way, Watson," Holmes said with confidence.

They moved towards the river, inspecting the warehouses as they went. Standing on the Shadwell Basin at the river's edge, Holmes rubbed his chin in contemplation. "Well, Watson, I didn't find what I was looking for. That means the access is inside one of these buildings. We'll take a closer inspection and see what they have for us."

Sherlock Holmes quickly eliminated several buildings that showed consistent activity. He was looking for a building that was or appeared to be abandoned. Three of those fit the description. After close examination, they found a boarded-up building that included the first and second floors with covered windows. The lock on the door had heavy rust and had not been tampered with for a year or more.

"Watson, I believe we have located the suspect's hiding place."

Watson looked at the bar-locked door, puzzled. "How does he enter if this is unused?"

"Elementary, my dear Watson. The door is meant to give the impression of abandonment, but there must be an alternate entry. Let's circle the building and see what we can find."

Holmes and Watson walked forty feet around the north corner into a narrow alley. A brick wall blocked them from circling any further, but stacked crates and used lumber were in a messy pile against the brick wall and building. A section of weathered and torn sail canvas draped over part of the bundle. Holmes pulled back the canvas and stepped behind, disappearing for a moment.

"Watson, we have found the entrance."

"Excellent, Holmes," Watson said as he took out his revolver.

Sherlock Holmes looked at the gun in Watson's hand and said, "There will be a right time for that, Watson. But for now, you can return it to your pocket."

"Are we not going inside? We might find the needed evidence to arrest the killer."

"Do you remember during our voyage on the Servia, I was able to detect how our suite had been gone through?" Holmes didn't wait for an answer. "I suspect the killer has the same sort of trip lines that would tip him off to our presence inside. But I have a plan for how to wrap up this nasty affair." Holmes turned and started for the street, saying to Watson, "Our next stop is to find Inspector Lestrade and enlighten him." Holmes was ten paces ahead before Watson followed while still trying to make sense of Holmes' comment.

The coach's driver was sitting at his station with his head on his chest, snoring softly upon their return. Holmes rapped on the side of the coach, and the driver's head jerked up, "Sorry, sir. A bit too much of Christmas cheer."

As they climbed in, Holmes ordered, "Take us to Scotland Yard."

"Yes, sir. Right away, sir." The driver took hold of the reins and said to the horses, "Walk on." Then, he made a U-turn in the street and headed west.

The desk sergeant sat reading a newspaper when Holmes and Watson came through the doors. Holmes moved through the lobby and stood at the counter, saying, "I would speak with Inspector Lestrade."

"I'm sorry, Mr. Holmes, the inspector, is still at home recuperating. But I can bring out Inspector Grayson if you would like to speak with him." The sergeant's eyes gave away his knowledge that this was the last thing Holmes would want.

Holmes slowly shook his head. "Please have someone inform Lestrade that I will be at home and expect him at his earliest convenience. I know he will come despite his condition."

"I believe you're right, Mr. Holmes. I will send for a carriage to the Inspector's residence and have him delivered within the hour, sir."

When Holmes and Watson were back in their coach, Watson asked, "Holmes? Why not just give them the information and be done with it?"

"If Lestrade is genuinely out of commission, that would leave the case to Inspector Grayson. He would undoubtedly bungle the case, and the killer would get away. Besides, I'm surprised the Inspector hasn't already shot himself in the foot by now."

"Another joke, Holmes? I'm not sure what to make of you," Watson chuckled.

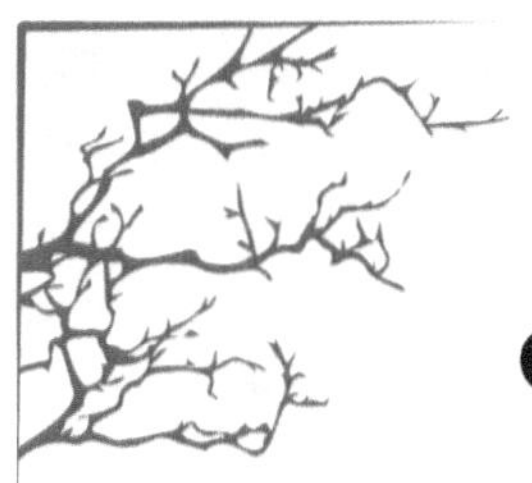

Chapter Thirty-Four

Sherlock Holmes had changed into his smoking jacket and was sitting by the fire with a glass of port when he heard the familiar footsteps of Inspector Lestrade bounding up the stairs.

"Watson, would you be so kind as to let the Inspector in and pour him a scotch? He will need it by the time I'm through."

Lestrade's knock was as heavy-handed as usual, considering his stature and wiry frame. "Good afternoon, Inspector," Watson said in greeting. "Come sit by the fire."

"Mr. Holmes, what news do you have for me? It must be vital for you to call me away from home," Lestrade said, sitting in a chair next to Sherlock Holmes and wiping his brow.

Holmes was never one to burst out with information. Instead, he took his pipe from the side table, packed the bowl, and lit it with three or four puffs.

"Holmes, you can be a most infuriating man sometimes," Lestrade said as Watson handed him his drink.

"How are you feeling, Inspector," Holmes said with a cloud forming over his head.

"Couldn't be better. Tell me why you asked me here before I come over there and shake it out of you." The Inspector's cheeks reddened.

"I assume there are those trained in bomb disposal at the Yard." Holmes' gaze moved from the fireplace to the Inspector.

Inspector Lestrade sat straight up in his chair. "A bomb? Where? And when was it placed?" the questions rolled rapidly off the Inspector's tongue.

"I'll answer the last question first. The bomb is in progress, and I figure the killer should have it rigged by the end of the day tomorrow. The where is the outside circumference of the dome at the National Gallery."

"Thank you, Holmes. We'll get right on it," the Inspector said, rising from his chair.

"Please sit down, Lestrade. I'm not finished yet." The Inspector did as asked. The killer is no fool. He has had Scotland Yard running around in circles for a year—that you cannot deny. This morning, I watched him gain access to the Gallery using documentation he created and then make his way to the roof to begin his placement of the explosives." Lestrade's eyes narrowed with the revelation.

Holmes continued, "He's too smart to get caught up there and has an escape route in reserve, much as he did at St. Paul's. So, you see, if you go storming up there, he will be gone before you open the roof door."

The Inspector stood and began pacing the room in long strides, "What are we supposed to do? We can't just sit on our hands until he commits another mass murder."

"That is precisely what I want you to do. Sit on your hands." Holmes gave his classic look when he was in total charge.

"Holmes, I've always thought that you were a bit eccentric, but now you sound like a lunatic," Lestrade waved his arms expressively in front of him.

Sherlock Holmes laughed. "If you will sit down, I will explain how to prepare for his capture. And in the end, you will be the toast of the town to a grateful public."

Inspector Lestrade huffed like an angry bulldog but acquiesced. "Alright, Mr. Holmes. Tell me your plans." All the bluster drained from the Inspector.

"Watson, I think the Inspector could stand a refill of his drink."

"We all could," Watson said as he went over to the liquor cabinet.

After the three gentlemen had their drinks in hand and seated again, Holmes explained, "There should be no alteration in the number of officers guarding the Gallery. He might notice even the slightest change. Next, we will wait until he has completed his installation and only disarm it on the eve of the event."

Inspector Lestrade interrupted, "Isn't that risky? He could set it off at any time."

"No, no, no. You need to understand, Lestrade. It isn't the destruction of the Gallery that he is fixated upon. It's the killing of a specific person who will be there on that night and in that exact location. It foiled his plans for the Christmas slaying when the intended priest died of natural causes. The killer learned of this event the same way I did when the gala's announcement appeared in the Times the other day. I anticipated his coming and have since located his place of hiding."

Sherlock Holmes spent the next half-hour making plans with the Inspector and what part the police would play in the final act.

The Inspector stood at the open entry door with his hat in hand. "Lestrade," Holmes stated, "I'm counting on you to be recouped and ready to do your part. So, go home and take care of yourself. And for God's sake, don't bring Grayson in on this, or he'll find a way to ruin our plans."

Lestrade slowly shook his head, "Don't worry, Holmes. Until it's time to disarm the explosives, I will keep this to myself." The Inspector turned and descended the stairs, walking gingerly and rubbing his head from a stunning headache.

THE KILLER HOOKED UP the last wire and slowly walked around the circumference of the dome, appreciating his handiwork. He then took a moment looking out over the city, from what some say is the highest point in London. The deep sense of pleasure welled up again, a self-induced high that only he could understand. Soon, the citizens of London would... His train of thought stopped cold. He neither knew nor cared what the citizens thought.

With a satisfied smile on his face, he gathered his tools, descended the stairs, and left the National Gallery.

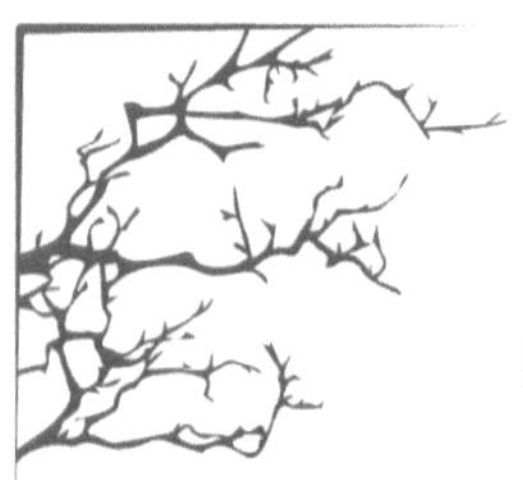

Chapter Thirty-Five

During the predawn hours, a squad of police officers enters the service entrance to the National Gallery. The security directed the eight men up several flights of stairs, and a guard unlocked the door to the roof. Four of these officers were specially trained in disarming explosives, taught when a faction of Irish dissidents started using timed explosives in their attempt to separate from England.

The remaining four officers would remain at their station, out of sight, for the next eighteen hours or until the suspect is captured.

The timing had to be just right to disarm the bombs. They didn't want any chance of being seen by the killer if he was keeping watch. They wouldn't use lanterns and waited until there was just enough morning light to do their delicate work. The officers crouched low to get into position. It amazed the lead officer that the suspect could have done this wiring and explosive placement with no one seeing his actions below. But then, there was continuous maintenance on this building, and why would anyone be curious? On his signal, the men stood up and began the process of disarming.

THE KILLER WAS SO PLEASED with his feminine disguise that he decided to attend the gala event dressed as a woman. He opened a bottle of Dom Perignon champagne and poured himself a glass. He then went throughout the warehouse and lit all the candles, including the unlit thirteenth symbolic candle, in celebration.

He spent the next hour perusing through several racks of clothing. It had to be just the right attire, appropriate for such an occasion, yet covering enough of him to hide his masculine features. It was simple to blend in when no one was taking notice. But this would be a well-attended party, and the female attendees would compare themselves to each other's wardrobe. He would be fashionable but demure.

The gown he chose was a silver brocade with long sleeves, frilled lace cuffs, and a high-clasped collar. The back was bustled to hide his features further. An added element to the dress was a close-fitted pocket that blended into the folds of the fabric where he would carry a Webley Bulldog pistol chosen for its compactness. He selected a pair of white lace-up shoes he had been stretching for months to fit his foot generally. Though it was a tight fit and uncomfortable, he would endure it willingly for this event.

INSPECTOR LESTRADE, Sherlock Holmes, and Dr. Watson stood in front of the bank on Cockspur Street, with the National Gallery towering in the distance.

"Our men are stationed on the roof, and we have chained the alternate routes off. If he comes up there, we'll have him in cuffs before he knows it," Lestrade said.

"And the Gallery?" Holmes asked.

"As you suggested, we will have a very visual presence at the start of the gala event with patrol officers in uniform. I'm having a dozen plain-clothed Inspectors dressed appropriately for the occasion. I intend to be there for the arrest, and I suppose you and Dr. Watson will also be in attendance?" Lestrade asked.

"No, Dr. Watson and I have other plans for the evening."

Surprised, Lestrade said, "After all the work you have put into his capture, I would have thought you and Watson would want to be the first to see him carted off in handcuffs."

Holmes smiled, "We will see, Inspector."

AS THE EVENING APPROACHED, the killer began his transformation process, starting with a close shave, being careful not to nick himself. Then, he sat in front of the mirror with an assortment of makeup. He applied lashes to his eyelids and used a razor to trim his brows. He added a flesh-tone paste to smooth out its features on his face. On top of that, he spread a thin layer of rouge to the cheeks. Eye shadow added just enough to accentuate his eyes.

He took a brown wig with set curls from a long counter and placed it on his head, completing that portion of his disguise.

Dreading this moment, he stepped into a corset and began drawing the laces. As they tightened, his shape gained a feminine curve at the waist. He inserted smallish balls of yarn at the chest to give himself the needed final curves.

When he was ready, he slipped into the gown and began buttoning up the back. He did have trouble reaching for the buttons only between the shoulder blades. With the collar hooked, it hid his Adam's apple, and the wig hid what was remaining of his masculine neck. Finished, he walked over to the mirror and appraised the end result.

It started with a smile as he scanned his torso. Stepping back, he took in the complete package and laughed, saying, "If Hillary was jealous before, she should see me now." The killer picked up the sides of the gown and twirled in circles, laughing hysterically.

A clock chimed the ninth hour, bringing the killer's attention back to the task at hand. He sat in his chair to put on the shoes, but he lifted the clock, looking at it and thinking of the little clock shop on Cross Street where he had taken it from. He closed his eyes, recalling the thrill that passed through his body as he watched the old man's life drain away.

He returned the clock to the side table, pulled on the first shoe, and laced up the ankle-length white satin strings. He felt the squeeze of his foot, and after four or five hours, he knew his feet would be sorely aching, but it would be worth every twinge of pain.

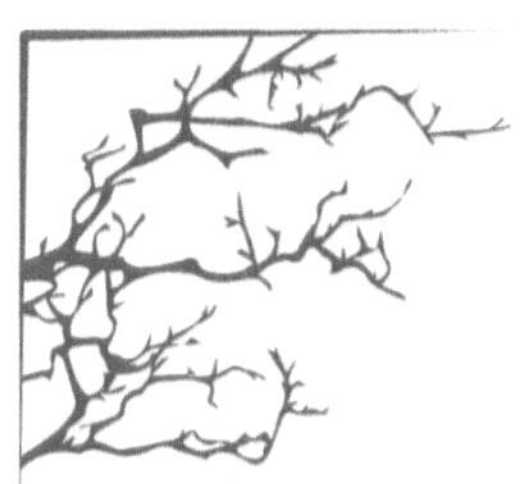

Chapter Thirty-Six

A full-length red cape trimmed in blue satin wrapped around the shoulders of the killer as he left the warehouse through the hidden door. He walked up Glamis Road, heading towards Cable Street, where he would hail a carriage. As he was crossing Juniper Row, a drunken man stepped out of the shadows and was about to block his way.

"Ello, pretty lady," he said, his breath overpowering with garlic and rum. His odoriferous body swayed like a tree in a storm.

The killer would have enjoyed slicing the throat of this foul creature, but he dared not spill blood on his clothes. Instead, he reached into his pocket and removed the hidden pistol, aiming it at the head of the offensive animal, and smiled at him.

Stunned, the drunk staggered backward and tripped over his own feet, falling hard on his back. With a guttural cry of pain, the drunk scrambled onto his knees and scurried off on all fours into the shadows like the dog he had become.

SHERLOCK HOLMES WAS finishing his pipe in front of the fire when he said, "Well, Watson, I believe it is about time we go." He stepped over to the fireplace and tapped out the ash in his pipe bowl.

"Alright, Holmes, I'll get my coat," Watson said, coming out of his bedroom.

"Watson, I think it best if you brought your revolver, just in case." Watson turned back to his room, opened the top dresser drawer, and lifted out the teak box containing his pistol. He checked the chambers to make sure they had been fully loaded.

"Do you have the candles, Holmes? Or should I get a few from the cabinet?"

"I've got them, Watson," said he.

The two men tread quietly down the stairs to avoid waking Mrs. Hudson. They exited the first-floor door into an empty street.

"Looks like it could be challenging to find a carriage at this hour," Watson said, buttoning his winter coat.

Holmes looked at his pocket watch without responding immediately. Then he moved closer to the curb and said, "Perhaps not, Watson."

A black coach with chestnut-colored horses trotted around the corner and stopped in front of them. Wordlessly, Holmes opened the cab door and climbed in, with Watson following behind.

"A bit of good luck, I would say," Watson said.

Sherlock Holmes laughed, "Not luck, Watson, planning. I had Lestrade send us this coach for this particular hour. After all, the devil is in the detail."

Lights were on in many windows, but the street was mostly empty. As they traveled along Fleet Street, they passed another carriage going in the opposite direction. Watson was sitting on the street side and noticed the single woman wearing a red cape with curly brown hair flowing over her shoulders. He wondered why an attractive woman would be alone traveling at this late hour of the night.

The carriage dropped Holmes and Watson several blocks from their destination and was asked to wait at the Vestry Hall off High Street until called by them.

The street lighting in this part of town was sparse. No moonlight penetrated through the overcast skies. Alleys were gaping black mouths of darkness and would give the faint of heart pause. Holmes and Watson moved through the dark street without lighting their candles until they arrived at the warehouse alley.

Sherlock Holmes took hold of Watson's arm, "We will have to enter very quietly. I don't expect him to be here, but if he is, I want to catch him unawares."

They cautiously moved through the ally, careful not to kick any debris. At the stacked pile, Holmes went in first, and in the blindness of the dark, he picked the lock.

THE KILLER'S CARRIAGE drew up to the National Gallery's broad steps behind a half dozen other coaches still de-boarding. He watched as dapperly dressed gentlemen held their hands up for the spectacularly dressed women with their dainty feet, stepping out onto the carriage step and being assisted to the cobblestone street.

The procession moved forward until it was his turn. He had almost made his first faux pas when his hand was on the inside door handle and about to exit on his own. But, taking a deep breath from his too-tight corseted lungs, he waited until the driver came and opened the door for him. With his gloved hand extended, the driver held it as he stepped down to the ground.

As the guests climbed the stairs, the steps were brightly lit with illumined candles. At the doors, each person was greeted and handed a brochure. When the killer stood at the threshold, he hesitated a moment, fearing his disguise would not pass scrutiny with the added security guards. He should not have been surprised by the hall full of uniformed police. This event would bring out the Who's Who in aristocratic society. But he put on a gay smile and crossed the lintel into the effervescent audience.

THE LOCK WAS FREED, and Holmes pushed on the well-oiled door. Pitch-blackness filled the room, and no sounds emanated. Sherlock Holmes listened to see if he could detect breathing, and a trap was prepared. When he felt satisfied, he reached out with his arm for Watson to follow.

Holmes closed the door and took out a candle from his jacket pocket, lighting it with a single match. He handed it to Watson and lit another one from the glowing flame.

Holmes and Watson moved through the warehouse to an area that appeared to be an apartment. The furniture seemed worn but comfortable. In the corner, near a stairway leading to the second floor, was a canopy bed with thick blankets and a silk duvet cover.

Holmes observed, "The furnishing was expensive at one time." Watson followed Holmes as they moved past this area.

Watson gasped when he caught sight of the rows of clothes racks. They walked up and down several aisles before Watson said, "There are more clothes here than a department store. But my question is, why all the women's clothing?"

"They're props, Watson. When I found him at the National Gallery, he came through the doors dressed as a woman and quite passable at that."

Watson suddenly had a dreaded thought: "Does Inspector Lestrade know the killer could be dressed as a woman?"

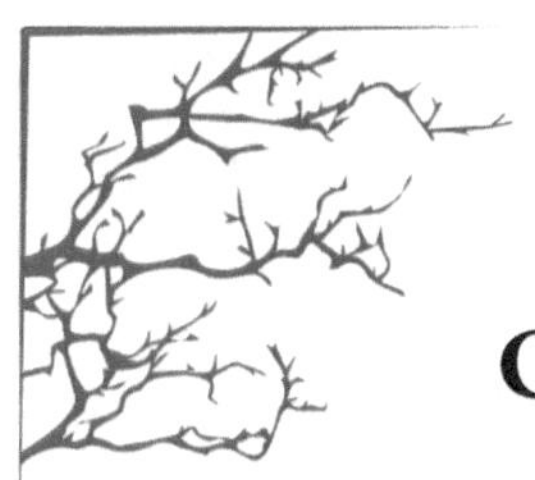

Chapter Thirty-Seven

Stewards were carrying trays of champagne on the main floor, and others had hors d'oeuvres for the guests as they mingled and made small talk. The killer stood transfixed as an attractive steward seemed to make a beeline towards him.

"Champagne?" he asked with a flirtatious smile.

The killer replied in a soft voice, "Thank you." He turned away as quickly as possible, walking to the far end of the room.

His mind raced. It worked, by God. Tension drained away, and he knew he could pull this off.

Only a few people were coming and going up the main stairs to the second level. He felt safe now, so he went to the upper floor to wait for the spectacular show he had planned. Conscious of eyes following him, he put on a feminine walk, glancing back at those watching. He smiled at them in full character.

"I INFORMED THE INSPECTOR that the killer could appear as anyone coming through the doors." Holmes looked his friend in the face, saying, "Watson, I don't expect Inspector Lestrade to capture the killer at the Gallery. At the stroke of midnight, his primary job is to surround the guest artist and escort him out of the reception room with as little fanfare as possible."

"What do you think the killer will do when he realizes they have disarmed the bombs, and they whisk his intended victim away right before his eyes?"

AT ELEVEN-FORTY-FIVE, the killer moved within twenty feet from the double doors to the octagonal hall. It would be at a relatively safe distance from his living Sodom and Gomorrah portrait when fire and brimstone would rain down on them.

As the hour approached, they offered him a second glass of champagne to toast the new year. Guests filtered into the room as a string quartet played Vivaldi's Winter movement of The Four Seasons.

Eleven-fifty-five, Inspector Lestrade, and three plain-clothed officers approach the guest of honor, "Excuse me, Mr. Marquez, I am Inspector Lestrade with Scotland Yard. Will you please follow us? We need to take you to a secured room."

"What are you saying? I don't understand. I have done nothing wrong." Marquez pleaded.

"There has been a threat to your life that is to be consummated at midnight. This way, please." The Inspector took the artist by his elbow and turned him away from the reception area.

Surrounded by the officers, Mr. Marquez was led to a pair of closed doors with two uniformed police standing guard. As they neared, the police officers opened the doors to let them through.

WITH ONE MINUTE TO midnight, the octagonal hall was packed. The killer sipped his drink, trying to hide the smile that was impossible to remove. His eyes caught every guest's movement as if they were dancing to a royal ball's stringed music.

Ten, nine, eight, he strained to find the honored artist in the crowd. Seven, six, he began to move closer, not wanting to miss his artistry. Five, four, a welling of alarm rose like bile. The victim was nowhere to be seen. Three, two, he resisted the urge to race into the room. One, his heart pounded in his chest. It felt like his ribs would crack at any moment.

The first chime struck; his ears expected a concussion. He involuntarily closed his eyes to protect himself from the imminent blast.

Happy New Year. Voices rang out as the quartet began playing Auld Lang Syne.

The killer became a stone statue, frozen in a millisecond in time. No explosion. The marble crystals in his brain refused to transmit. Cold sweat formed on his face as he came to. His first impulse was to draw his pistol, charge into the room, and shoot Jesus Marquez in the head. But his own need for survival held him back.

Slow, tentative steps, he walked into the room, a specter unseen by the happy revelers. He moved about in a fog. Was he looking for Marquez? Or an explanation? Hot, passionate rage kindled within. All pretense of character gone, he turned away and ran, bumping into others as he made for the stairway caught up in a tornado, taking leaps downward. He slammed through the entrance doors, knocking an elderly gentleman to the ground.

The killer almost stumbled down the dew-covered stone exterior steps. Running to the waiting carriage, he shouted, "Go," he said as he jumped aboard.

The driver whipped the horses in a state of confusion. The woman he had taken suddenly spoke in a definitely masculine voice. His preordained instructions were to drop his fare at the corner of Cable and Charles Street. A commission he was anxious to complete.

DR. WATSON HAD LONG ago found a crate to sit upon. He and Holmes had extinguished their lights for what seemed to be hours. He marveled at how his senses altered with the lack of candlelight. His pupils expanded, and each vestige of ambient light showed like a beacon. The sense of smell heightened, and he could hear Holmes breathe fifteen feet away.

Sherlock Holmes had told him to remain at his position upon the return of their suspect and to be ready to respond to the evolving circumstances.

THE HORSES SOON LATHERED from their race across the empty city. Their breath fogged their faces as they came to a stop at the appointed location. A hand from inside the coach pushed open the carriage door before the driver could dismount. The fare jumped to the street and disappeared into the shadows.

"Git," the driver shouted, his whip snapping above the ears of the horses. The carriage lunged forward, picking up speed as the driver took a deep breath of relief.

WATSON HEARD A DISTANT echo of running footfalls that became clearer each moment. They stopped quickly and then came the sound of scuffing feet on steps. These sounds made no sense in this context, and he wondered if he had just imagined them.

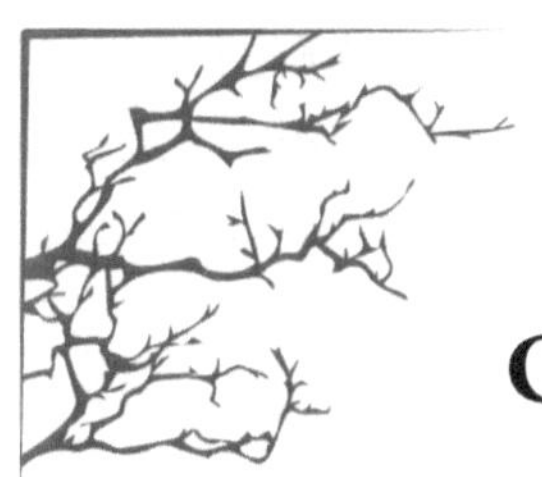

Chapter Thirty-Eight

A clank of metal and creaking of wood brought Watson's attention into complete focus. From an unexpected location, a crack of light illuminated the floor. A flooring section seemed to levitate before a hand appeared holding a metal ring. The light grew stronger as a candle came into view. At first, a face glowed by the candle, then more of the body appeared as the killer climbed the last steps.

The appearance of the woman he'd seen in the carriage on their way to the warehouse stunned Watson. He started to take a step forward but caught himself.

The killer set his candle on the counter and yanked the wig off his head, throwing it on the floor. Watson saw Sherlock Holmes step out of the shadows, and he started to follow suit.

It momentarily caught the killer off guard. He reached into his pocket, and with one quick motion, he pulled out a pistol and fired at Holmes. But in doing so, the barrel had snagged the fabric, and his shot missed the intended mark, striking Holmes on the right side of his chest.

Before the killer could aim for Holmes' heart, Watson raised his revolver and fired at his forearm, causing him to lose his gun. "Do not move," said I, "or I'll be forced to aim for a more vital organ."

Sherlock Holmes slumped against the counter with a sheen of sweat forming on his brow. Watson quickly subdued the suspect with a piece of cord he had picked up before dimming his candle earlier.

At his friend's side, he examined the wound. The bullet had passed through his back, and he bled from both openings. Grabbing a white shirt within arm's reach from the rack, Watson tore it in half, placing one piece on his back. "Holmes, hold this," he said as he staunched the bleeding from the chest wound.

Holmes asked, "Where is Anthony Colton?"

"I have him tied up to the pipe against the wall." Watson pointed him out to Holmes. "I'm almost finished. You take the gun, and I'll get the driver here so I can get you to Bart's Hospital." Holmes nodded his head in acknowledgment.

ANTHONY COLTON SAT in the cab between the two men who had ruined his life. They spoke quietly to each other and used their names back and forth. The names of Sherlock Holmes and Dr. Watson would forever be branded into his memory. Even now, he fantasized about the terrible and wondrous deaths they would experience. He was so lost in his thoughts that he forgot about the pain from the gunshot wound.

MID-MORNING ON THE third floor of Bart's, Holmes laid in his bed wishing he had asked Watson to bring him his pipe. If he were going to be trapped here, he would need the distraction. The window in the room faced a brick wall, and Holmes hoped a bird would take perch on the sill. At least that would give him something to watch.

Dr. Watson stood a moment at the open room door, watching Holmes stare out the window. "It's not The Langham Hotel, is it, Holmes?" Watson said as he stepped inside.

Sherlock Holmes began to laugh but stopped quickly, grabbing his chest at the wound site. "No, and they don't serve the same food here either," he said, smiling.

Watson moved a chair up to the bed, "Let's have a look at those wounds." He turned back the sheet and examined them. "Not bad stitch work."

"They should be. I have a pretty good doctor. I'll give a reference for him if you like." Watson smiled broadly at the compliment. "So, Doctor, when do I get out of here?"

Watson shook his head, "I knew you would be a lousy patient."